HEROES

VOLUME 1: SHINING IN THE SHADOWS

BY KATIE MAJOR

Text copyright © 2014 Katie Major

Dedicated to the wonderful and unwavering love and support of my mother without whom this book would not be here

Just because we don't like it, does not mean it is wrong…..

Prologue

WHAM!!

I landed on the other side of the kissing gate at the end of the lane. The screams of tyres, horns blasting and shouts made my head snap around.

A black cab.

A smashed windscreen.

A flow of blood.

A body.

My father's body.

Silence.

Stillness.

Chapter 1

I am Fenn. I am 30 years old and for the first time in fifteen years I am permitted to have a pen. It is a simple black pen with the usual transparent plastic casing and a brass coloured ball point, so nothing particularly special and very cheap. But it writes. The ecstasy of anticipation and desire almost hurts because I cannot remember the last occasion on which I wrote, let alone what it was that I wrote. Perhaps, it was at school. I have imagined what I should like to write on such a day and I have envied the other girls with their felt pens, glitter pens and big chunky marker pens, even their lipsticks were capable of expression. In group sessions, I was watched closely by them and their pens and pencils were carefully steered away from me by the monitors. And now I stare at the pen. I feel my eyes burn and flare at the incalculable possibilities. The social worker in turn glares at me.

"Is everything okay?" She demands.
I nod, head bowed.
"Well, shall we start?" She suggests pointedly that she has better things to do than to baby-sit me.
Her duty is to assist me to reintegrate myself back into society- so far as I am permitted.
"I am here to help you to complete all the necessary

paperwork, to attend the required interviews and to obtain the vital information. I will also be required to take you to places- shops, restaurants, parks, the zoo - highlighting those establishments to which you may go to and those which are subject to strict prohibitions."

The coolness in her manner suggests this is some way off; her slight frame, looking awkward in her slightly oversized suit in a way that hints at a desperately rapid loss of weight, is pressed firm against the back of the chair, which is set back away from the table. Her shining hair is cut precisely; it lies square along her jaw line and is parted severely in the centre so that the dark, almost black colour seems harsh against the paleness of her skin. The black square eyeglasses that are pressed onto the bridge of her nose reflect my own poor appearance. The suit is a dark colour, perhaps navy or black; the sunlight makes it difficult to distinguish from where I am sitting. My attention is drawn to a small silver badge affixed to the lapel of her jacket, which seems to form the shape of a blazing sun. A memory of this little badge seems to resonate in the depths of my subconscious and it starts to irk me that I can't place it.

She sits directly opposite me, across this arid expanse of pine. We are sitting in the kitchen, a bright, warm and welcoming room that is large, open but still crammed with all the equipment I'll probably never need.

"You will no doubt be aware that the President considers you to be dangerous and a threat to our national security. Consequently there are various restrictions." He voice is plain but yet full of pompous self righteousness. I want to scream.

I have long since accepted that I will not ever truly be released by my captors and that the accommodation I am now afforded is simply a means of ensuring that they continue to retain control over me; there are closed circuit cameras at the front door, at the back door and in the garage of this small cottage in the suburbs. I know that the click when I pick up the telephone means a recording is made somewhere of whatever is said on the line so I use all my efforts to ensure that I give them no reason to use such evidence against me.

"The cottage has two bedrooms, a bathroom, kitchen and lounge area. A short drive leads to a garage and there is a small walled garden to the rear of the property. The kitchen is at the back of the house." I was told by the Estate Agent as I was lead around. Now, the windows behind the kitchen sink have a full view of the square patio which is surrounded by two lengths of brightly colourful flowerbeds and two broad strips of lush vividly green grass. An iron table with a pair of matching chairs glistens with the early morning freshness in the centre of the patio. A towering brick wall is covered with a deep layer of ivy but I can still see the razor wire poking out of the top of the shiny green leaves.

A small cough drags my wavering attention back to the kitchen and the table.

"I don't have all day. I have other NV's like you to deal with today." Her voice is tight as she fingers the little sun. A knot grows in my stomach as a small amount of acidic liquid gathers at the bottom of my throat.

Anyway, she is searching. She looks puzzled and bemused. Where is the evil? She wonders. It could never have been obvious because I have never felt it. But it must have been there else the last fifteen years would never have happened. Or would it? She doesn't understand me. She doesn't understand my experience. I doubt that she even wants to try.

And then I look at the forms, islands neatly placed on the sea of the pine table. They are printed with lots of spaces and boxes; no room for ambiguity or deviation. I have taken a deep breath, the sort you've taken when you're diving for something precious lost at the bottom of a pool, as if your lungs are about to burst, and then I press the pen to the page, breaking the tense surface. I finish printing my name; eons have passed and I feel a surge of power through my spine and along my shoulders. My fingers tingle from the excited and crazed messages they are receiving from my battered mind. My poor mind that has been constrained and repressed is unable to think expansively, rather it has been forced into a narrow passage like waste water directed through drains and sewers, left to fester with the rats and putrid decomposed rubbish racing alongside.

"That wasn't too difficult, want it?" She surmises, a nasty smile appearing.

I have three tasks to complete today; my voting application, a job application and my letter.

After his historic third term of election, the President advised his public that all individuals would have to apply for their vote. In writing. His reasoning was that those who could write could better understand politics and ergo what he wanted to achieve; he wanted a better quality of voter and, above all, He wanted to protect his position by what effectively encouraged voter apathy. His public argument; that if the Vote was limited, people would cherish it and use it wisely, which would actually reverse the declining Voter turnout.

His plan worked. He's been in power since before I was born. The "Vote Form" seems complicated, involved and probing. I will have to practice first. They say that the form is designed to test your command of language but I can tell that what they really mean to do is to consider your values and beliefs through your sentences, paragraphs, phrases and words in the limited space afforded to you by the boxes on the forms. They analyse your handwriting to see deep into your thoughts, through the gateway to your personality. And then they decide whether you should be able to vote, and whether you will need assistance in future. Assistance that only the Government is able to provide.

Roughly speaking, all citizens of age are now separated into three categories upon their application; Free Voters, Assisted Voters and Non Voters. Anyone who displays or expresses any difference in opinion to the Government becomes a Non Voter unless, subsequent to the Governmental Voting Commission's efforts, they agree to become an Assisted Voter. All Assisted Voters are monitored to check their affiliations continue as agreed by the Commission, but there are a few perks such as the ability to purchase stamps, stationery, send email and mix with whomever the Assisted Voter desires (subject to an approved list submitted monthly to the Commission.) Non Voters are prohibited from having email at home, from having post delivered to their home address (they have to collect it and sign for it at the Local Commissioners' office if they receive any at all) and their movements are monitored continuously and closely. Free

Voters are citizens who have signed statutory declarations affirming their loyalty to the President, simply waiting for approval by the bestowal of citizenship upon them and are effectively permitted to do as they please. I have no doubt that my application is futile; I will remain a Non Voter forever.

I was 24, and in confinement, when this concept was introduced, and it is now settled law, much to the consternation of external observers. The UN has given up monitoring our so-called elections, they take the view that at least we are a peaceful nation and we don't try to kill each other. So I am to take my chances because not to accept this fate will raise more questions, I will complete the form as I am expected to do.

Another cough. I must press on.

So I will write my answers out first and then copy them when I am happy. Will I be happy? I guess I shall find out.

Chapter 2

My early life passed happily as I flourished in my role as the focus of my parents' attention. It was a part I eagerly assumed and played with relish and accomplishment. I allowed my parents to dote. Everything I wanted I was given, whether it was food or toys or even a kind word. If I am frank, it didn't even have to be kind. I should have been content, but I was a leech, greedily sucking at the source of the attention, and as addicts, my parents relinquished all their resistance to the temptation I offered to them.

So by the time I was twelve, I was busy. I was learning the piano, attending ballet lessons and engaging with my new peers at my school. St Catherine's enjoyed a reputation for educating the young ladies who would emerge from its doors with elegance, dignity and a sense of duty in all aspects of life; socially, politically and academically. The school was a cruel looking building, ancient and dark, with turrets and battlements that bore gargoyles, watching passers by from every corner. The ceilings were high, the beech floors were polished and the oak doors heavy. The sense of authority that permeated into the rooms from the oak panelled walls did not mute the spirits of my cohorts, rather it served as bait for our tricks as we felt urged to laugh and giggle, swap secret notes and whisper rude messages amongst ourselves during lessons and assemblies. We compared our notes, satchels and houses; we tried on each others' shoes, tied each others' hair and grew up together. We shared all the experiences of our pubescent development and yielded our angst ridden thoughts to comfort, resolution and ridicule.

Louisa was my closest friend, and it was more than convenient that our mothers were members of the same health club. Louisa would come round to visit at least twice a week and I to her house as often. Frequently, we would be invited to stay for dinner. Our mothers even knew our particular dietary requirements in that I didn't much care for green vegetables so wouldn't touch them but Louisa found carrots disagreeable and her mother didn't serve them. If green vegetables wandered onto my plate, it was as if my throat would swell with buboes and my stomach wretch like a whip lashing against the herd. Miraculously, though, my greens were always finished and my plate left clean whilst Louisa's detested carrots were all consumed at the same time. Our parents were relaxed about dinner, as long as we called to let them know. It was common courtesy after all, as was the message drilled into us at school and at home.

Our games would vary. We would dress up, raid the make up drawers and totter on our mothers' heels. It is amazing to think that neither of us did any damage to our ankles in those fashionable stilts. Sometimes, in the hot lazy summers, we would idle away hours in the late afternoon sunshine haring around on our bikes in the local parks.

We could get to the park through the coolness of a long, leafy lane that ran alongside our house, the same one my grandmother and I had used years previously. It was a grey, gravel track over which willow trees growing on either side almost met to create a light, airy but strangely cool tunnel that opened up into a sun-bathed, expansive meadow with softly rolled grassy undulations. An avenue of oak trees lined up down the middle of the meadow, through which a smooth tarmac pathway found its way to a crystal clear river, gently trickling over the rocks and stones that were nestled at the bottom. We would congregate at a small stone beach at the end of the avenue of trees; our bikes would be casually and carelessly tossed down on to the river bank. Hours were carelessly abandoned to history as we stood in the cool water, letting it flow over our toes. We sat still on the bank, dangling our legs into the watery abyss as we observed the local toads, sticklebacks and water voles fighting to maintain their existence despite the attentive and curious efforts of the native comprehensive schoolboys whom we would determinedly ignore with flirtatious indifference.

"Yawn, I've got to go to my Nana's tonight" moaned Louisa, on one of our trips.
"That's okay, isn't it?"
"Nah, she's in a home that smells awfully and she just rambles on about old stuff that I don't understand. It's so boring."
"She must be bored by herself?" I offered.
"I guess so. It just all seems so irrelevant." Louise yawned and

stared at her nails, I looked away to avert my watery eyes, thinking with desperate sadness of my own grandmother.

"Where are your grandparents?" Louisa's demanding voice snapped me out of my introspection.

"All died."

"Oh."

"I miss my grandmother so much. She was so special- we spent lots of time together reading, playing, telling each other stories. Her imagination was wonderful".

"My mum says that imagination gets people into trouble." Louise said.

"Why?" I asked.

"Well you can't control someone's imagination, can you?" Louise retorted with a snort.

Once there had been an ancient bench, of the type that had stone pillars and sturdy planks of wood, perhaps it had once had a tribute to some much loved lost one. Time and the weather had constantly eaten away at the planks of wood so that only the stone pillars remained, covered in slimy green moss. Still, they were often useful for leaning our bikes against if we felt like being careful. The bench had been just about fit for purpose when my grandmother and I would wander down to the stream to read our books and indulge in our secrets.

"So what book have you brought today, Grandma?" I asked

eagerly.

"I haven't, but I thought I'd tell you one of my own."

"Really? Cool."

"Once upon a time there was a princess. She was very beautiful with long, shiny black hair."

"What kind of dress was she wearing?"

"A pink dress that the reached the floor, with lots of lace and netting so that it swished as she walked."

"That sounds lovely, did she have a tiara?"

"Yes, it was silver and had lots of tiny diamonds which sparkled in the sunshine."

"oooooh."

"Well, the Princess had a father who was the King of all the land, and he loved the Princess very much. She was his only daughter and the King wanted only the very best for her. He didn't want her to be corrupted."

"What does that mean?"

"He didn't want her turned bad."

"Oh, okay."

"So he stopped her from leaving the Castle grounds."

"Was it a big castle?"

"Yes, it had had hundreds of rooms. All the beds were four poster beds and had beautiful richly coloured tapestries draped over them. The windows were all stained glass in a rainbow of colours. "

"Did it have a big garden?"

"The biggest! In fact, the Castle had many gardens within its high stone walls- one for flowers, one for croquet and others for vegetables and fruit, so the Princess had acres and acres around which she could wander. However, she could always see the Castle and its walls and so she never forgot that he world was self contained. She would sit in the Castle and stare at the world outside of the Castle walls- farmers' wives hustling around the market, young men falling out of the pubs and children kicking a football around in the street. There seemed to be so much going on that the Princess got curious and asked her father, what was outside of the Castle gates. The King, afraid of what might happen if he told her of the wonderful things outside of the Castle, lied to her and told her that the world was full of horrible people who didn't like her and wanted her dead. He told her that no-one could be trusted but reassured her that he would look after her."

"That's not very nice Mummy tells me that you should never lie."

"Yes, that's right and you should always remember that." My grandmother answered me patiently, seemingly unbothered by my interruptions.

"So what happened?"

"The Princess cried and cried. She couldn't believe that the happy ladies in the market who sometimes waived to her would want to do her harm. Now, the Queen had watched her daughter blossom into a beautiful young woman and agreed that she needed protection, but now she saw that her daughter had become sad and worried. The Princess didn't talk to anyone- she stayed inside and stopped smiling at all the servants. The Queen thought that the King had gone too far and decided that she needed to talk to him."

My grandmother paused for break and I looked expectantly up at her, ready for the drama to unfold.

"Well, when the Queen spoke to the King, he flew into a terrible rage. He was the King and he knew what was best. How dare the Queen question his authority! He banned the Queen from talking to the Princess about this and ordered the servants to spy on the Queen and tell him if she broke the rules. The Queen knew it was no good and felt helpless as the King banned the staff from leaving the Castle. The Princess sat at the window of her bedroom which was in the tallest tower of the Castle. She couldn't see what the King was so worried about."

"Was the King a bad man?"

"Not really. He just didn't want anything to happen to the Princess. He thought he knew best but he didn't realise that he was making her so unhappy. His lies had been persuasive but from her perch in the Castle tower the Princess couldn't see what was so wrong with life outside of the Castle. On her occasional walks around the grounds of the Castle, she would often end up at the river, which flowed through the grounds at the very edge of the Castle estate. The King hadn't seen fit to build walls along the river because he felt that the river provided adequate protection as it was very deep and fast flowing. Many fishermen had drowned after falling in and the locals believed that the river was cursed, a curse that the King relied upon for protection. As the months and years passed, the Princess watched the River, getting increasingly frustrated and desperate in her confinement."

"Did she get bored?"

"Yes, very even though the King arranged for the servants' children to come and entertain her. He thought that they would not be able to tell her about life on the outside when they sang and danced for the Princess."

"What songs did they sing?"

"Only ones that the King had approved."

"Well that's no fun!"

"Exactly, so the Princess suggested that they play hid and seek."

"What a great idea. With all those gardens there would be hundreds of hiding places!!" I exclaimed.

"She sent all the children off to hide, knowing that she had explored all of the possible hiding places in the Castle grounds. In half an hour she had found all but one of the children."

"Wow!"

"Well the Princess was very puzzled by this and after another hour she still couldn't find the other child. She was starting to get worried so she asked the other children to help her. Suddenly, a shout went up! The last child had been found by the river- hiding in the roots of a tree which overhung the river. An idea came to the Princess as she peered through the roots and into the meadow beyond. When the children had left and the King and Queen had gone to bed, she stole some old clothes from her maid and crept through the roots in the tree. Pulling herself up, she looked around the grassy meadow and saw a path, lit by the moon that headed into the town."

"I bet she was scared." My interjection was earnest in its sincerity.

"Yes, she was. It was very dark and the Princess didn't know anyone. As she came into the town, she tried to hide in the shadows, hoping no one would see her. The market place was deserted- the stalls empty of their goods and rubbish littering the floor but some movement underneath one of the stalls caught the Princess' eye. She followed the motion and was surprised to see a young woman creeping beneath the stalls- eventually emerging close to the Princess. The Princess was even more shocked to see that the young woman had a bag, full of scraps that she had collected from the floor beneath the stalls and the Princess made to run back to the Castle as the young woman glanced at her. The young woman called out to her and the Princess stopped; they began to talk under the clear starry night and it became apparent that they were very different. The Princess had everything she wanted except freedom and the young woman had nothing else but her freedom. Neither was very happy and envied each other so they agreed to swap places for a week. The Princess spent the next week scratching about on the floor of the market, creeping into barns to sleep and washing in cattle troughs. She watched the people closely- laughing, shouting, fighting, talking and realised how lucky they were to live without constraint. Meanwhile, in the Castle, the King realised quickly what had happened and banished the young woman into exile."

"What's exile?"

"Well, it means being sent to another place and being told that you can't come back because if you do something very bad will happen."

"But that wasn't very fair!" I protested at the injustice.

"I know but the King was very angry and didn't know where the Princess was. Word spread quickly about what had happened, so much so that whilst wandering around out the back of a pub, the Princess overheard two grooms talking about it. She was shocked at what her father had done and swore never to go back. The King never saw his daughter again and it was said that he died of a broken heart."

"That's really sad. What happened to the Princess?"

"Well, she eventually met a young groomsman who took her in gave her clothes and somewhere to live and eventually they got married."

"And the young woman?"

"I don't know because she never returned from exile." My grandmother looked down at me with sadness in her eyes. "Did you learn anything from my story?"

"Yes, you can't keep people locked in Castles with lies." I said bluntly. My grandmother smiled with satisfaction and nodded sagely as she took my grubby little hand to steer me home.

Looking back, I recall with clarity another moment when I realised that I was "different" from the others. It was a usual Saturday morning at the Health Club and Louise and I were having our nails done. My grandmother had passed away only weeks before and her death was still raw for me. I hadn't yet accepted her permanent absence from my life and there was a huge yawning gap for me that I thought I would never again fill.

"Hmmmm. Red, black or purple?" I mused over the range of colours on offer.

"You know we're not supposed to have any of those!" Louise reproached me.

"Yeah well, what's my mother going to do about it?" My tone was challenging and aggressive.

"You'll get into so much trouble, you'll probably get grounded. Don't forget it's Olivia's birthday next week!"

"Exactly, I'll have cool nails for the party."

"You reckon? They'll remove it before school on Monday!"

"C'mon, it'll be fun."

"No, it won't, not when we get into so much trouble." Louise turned away haughtily and let her nailed be painted with clear nail varnish.

I smile as I remember that she was right. My mother had a fit when she saw the black nail polish, which was forcibly removed as soon as we got home.

Chapter 3

So it was Louisa who went shopping with my mother and I before our first social. The Social was the event of the spring term. Now we were fifteen, it was deemed appropriate for us to meet like-educated and similarly groomed gentlemen who had properly directed professional ambitions. I think the idea was that it would develop our social skills, without fear of scandalous repercussion. I find the naiveté of the old puzzling when I consider that in theory they have been there and thought about it and often carried it out before the young were even born.

My grandmother once told me a story about her youth- shortly before she died. It was the day she gave me my most prized possession and I was 13.

She had grown up in the same village in which she had brought up my mother; her father was a farmer and it was her job to deliver eggs to the locals. As my mother did later with cakes, she would place the eggs in the basket of the bicycle and carefully ride around the dusty lanes, visiting the neighbours.

"I always left the Jones house to the very end." She said with a sparkle in her eye, mischievous and childlike.

"Really Grandma, why was that?"

"A young man."

"Oh really, was it Grandpa?"

"Oh no. He came along much much later." She closed her eyes, revealing her paperlike eyelids, frail and delicate in her advancing years. I could see her picture the scene in her mind.

"Luke was beautiful. A year older than me, he often came to help father with the harvest."

"So come on, stop teasing, what did he look like?"

"Tall, tanned, dark hair that went reddish in the summer with sparking green eyes. Oh and very muscular." She smiled and her face lit up, she giggled at the memory. "He was always smiling and laughing, usually at my curly red hair, before he could get close enough to pull my pigtails. Now every Friday night, we had a music night for the youngsters in the village at the Church Hall. A live band would play and the parents would take it in turns to chaperone us. One night, Luke had sneaked in some of his parent's homemade cider and a group of us hid outside in the dark yard, swigging from this green glass bottle. The stars were watching and twinkling at us. Suddenly I realized that all the others had crept back into the hall and that it was just Luke and I, by which time I had started on a cigarette that someone else had acquired from home. Luke and I shared this cigarette, moving ever closer together until it was impossible to avoid a kiss. Our lips had just touched, Luke's hand pressed to the small of my back, but then the door burst open." My grandmother sighed dramatically. "And Luke and I broke apart, turning to face my mother of al people! I'd never seen her in such a fierce rage- she was angry at me for a full week. I couldn't tell if it was the kissing, the cigarette or the cider!!" She finished her story with a chuckle.

Curious, I prodded a little further. "So what happened to Luke?"

"Well like your grandfather he was shipped off to war, but unlike your grandfather, he never came back." A darkness passed across her face and she drifted off back into her memories.

Anyway, the social was a fantastic excuse to extort new outfits and to defraud our parents of shoes, haircuts and nail polish. Each member of the gang had chosen a colour and we all swore a solemn oath not to renege on our agreement, breach of which would cause social embarrassment for us all. After much protestation, and animated discussion amongst us all, I had settled on black.

My mother had accepted my choice as if I had said that I had wanted chips for dinner and my father had merely muttered that "black wasn't really the colour for my little girl". At this my mother just rolled her eyes in an arc, in my direction although clearly in full view of my father who then quickly retreated to his shell, having ventured his opinion. I remember my father had been in the kitchen, stooped over a forest of papers on the table and his laptop computer, when my mother and I had updated him as to our- rather my- intentions towards our forthcoming shopping expedition.

"First, Daddy- are you listening? - Mummy says we can go to that big posh department store in Knightsbridge and, if we can't find anything there, we'll go to Regent Road." I pranced precociously in front of my father.
"Street, darling". He corrected me. My father peered up at my mother with his glasses perched perilously at the end of his nose.
"Really? Oh, okay, Regent Street," I reminded myself with the purpose of a typist correcting her letters. My father returned to his papers. The creases in his brown tensed, deepening like crevices in a glacier. My father didn't work in the kitchen as a rule as that was my mother's sovereign territory in which she

would bake pies for school, cakes for the reading club, wash all my clothes- uniform and all- iron those clothes and force me to eat my breakfast along with a whole list of other motherly type activities with which I wasn't entirely familiar but were nevertheless pinned to the notice board with an allocated time and day. I didn't trust my father as he seemed to be engrossed in the numbers spread out across the kitchen table.

"And we'll spend hundreds of pounds on my outfit for the social to make sure that I am the prettiest there!" I announced my sincerely held intentions with gusto.

My father slowly raised his head and brought his eyes up to meet my mother's. A nervous, brusque and brief glance towards my mother that should have been telling, however I was too deep into my imaginary world of black mini dresses, patent high heels and pink lipstick to read the intricacies of non-verbal communication between adults. My mother asked me to go to the toilet and to put my shoes on before we left to pick up Louisa. Her voice was commanding, no room for misunderstanding or disobedience in her short sharp orders that I dared not disobey.

I ran up the stairs two at a time and slammed all the doors as I went; the interior plaster walls reverberated with elephantine force. I didn't have time for this, I was high on the anticipation of looking sexy and grown up and now had to have a pee, get my coat and shoes from the bedroom and get back downstairs as soon as possible. I ran clumsily between the toilet and my bedroom, waded down the stairs as I shoved my arms into my coat and feet into shoes, octopus like in my haste. I landed on the door mat and scrambled to my feet, yelling "Ready now!" at the top of my voice.

Silence returned my call.

But not quite.

I strained to hear any sound of movement from the kitchen and caught the sounds of a current of murmurs. Hushed voices ebbed under barrier of the closed door, and then the murmurs retreated again. I caught odd words, the even ones sailed away out of earshot forever.
"….failed to spot it?"
"Receivers went in yesterday……staff sacked…… bills unpaid…… not see that again…"
I craned my neck towards the door, not yet daring to leave the door mat.
"And the mortgage?" My mother stammered. She was nervous. I know that as a girl she had had a terrible speech impediment, which by a mixture of treatments and her marriage to my father had been temporarily cured. This was

only the third time I had heard it and I had already learned that it meant she was scared.

On the first occasion I heard this stammer, I had been treated to a day out to a theme park whilst on holiday in the United States- before the sanctions were put it into effect of course- and I had begged my father to take me on one of the fiercest roller coasters in the world at the time. I was nine and my diminutive frame meant that I had only just peaked over the rigorously enforced height restriction. My mother had vehemently argued with my father over the issue and as the dispute progressed, her stammer had deteriorated to such an extent that she didn't sound like herself, rather like a toy robot whose batteries are dying. It had frightened me; this wasn't my normally calm and placid mother. Each syllable was delayed, being forced through a sieve. As each word became more difficult, the next one would become near impossible, her face reddening and her hands wrestling with her unbearable frustration, working in agitating circular motions.

I could only imagine what she was doing now on the other side of the door, but as I did so, a shadow passed from left to right and back again under the door.

"Couldn't see this coming..."
"Shock......we'll make cut backs.......have to make

allowances…..Fenn, this Friday…!"

I could hear the urgency in my father's throat, forcing his voice into a serenity that seemed unnatural and out of place in the seemingly volatile hostility of the kitchen. I could fee the tension radiate through the crack under the kitchen door. My mother, despite her stammer, was using all her powers to dispel the despair from her voice, trying to keep it quiet enough so that their conversation would be private. I slid my shoes off my feet and stepped across the carpet towards the kitchen door, as I lifted my foot for a second step, a huge crash emanated from the kitchen like a belch; a plate of something had been knocked to the floor. I jumped back to the sanctuary of the door mat.

Suddenly the doorbell rang, like a siren, loud and clear.

It transpired that Louisa's mother had thought it easier if she brought Louisa around to our house as she was on her way to the Health Club anyway. It seemed that my face betrayed me as Mrs West said "Fenn? Whatever is the matter? You're very pale."
I forced a smile and replied that I felt fine, and didn't know why I might look that pale, but thanked her all the same for her concern. At least school had taught me something, even if it was to lie particularly well. Behind me the kitchen door had

swung open and my parents strode out, smiling, in fact beaming. Broad smiles emblazoned across their faces. Confusion slapped me in the face; my mother should be red eyed and shaking and my father tense, silent and morose. That is what they were usually like after fights. Why was this so different?

In all the fuss, I had popped my shoes back on and was ready to leave. My mother swung her handbag over her shoulder and announced we were off, briefly exchanging pleasantries with Mrs West at the same time. She smacked my father across the cheek with her kiss and strode across the drive to the car leaving Louisa and I trailing in her wake. The stammering, stop-starting state that my mother had been in had vanished to the point that she now seemed peaceful and relaxed. The fog of confusion had been dissipated by the excitement of Louisa arriving but the anxiety and bewilderment born out of my parents' fight still lurked at the back of my mind, in the shadows of my memory, a moth-eaten hat at the back of the wardrobe. Sprawled decadently across the luxury of the back seat of my mother's Range Rover, Louisa and I were a pair of chaffinches, chattering away. My mother brought the car to a slow cumbersome stop, the weight of the vehicle resisting my mother's foot.

In the elephantine vehicle we were high enough to see the

gathered crowds outside the stately Town Hall in the grey, misty rain. Placards, banners and surges of faces pressed forward towards the steps as the Police lined the road, trying to force traffic onwards. The faces, disfigured with hatred, contorted by anger were driving themselves hard upon the steel barriers in an attempt to breach the protection set up by the Police. Calling, cursing, chanting and crying out words I could hardly make out as the sounds broke upon the deaf walls of the Town Hall amongst the ravaging anarchy. Articulation was vague as one syllable merged into the next, and had it not been for the bright, undulating forest of banners I would have remained ignorant of this cause. Words like "freedom", "individual", "censorship" and "clone" pierced the tension between the crowd and its restraints. "Free our Minds" pleaded one isolated placard among the throng of bodies and limbs; another "My Soul, My Choice". There was a thud against the window as pink flesh, pockmarked as if it had been tenderised with a steak hammer, was pressed against the glass of the car. The lone, green eye that I could see turned to me. It looked at me and seemed to peer directly into my brain.

"Don't let them tell you what to think." The man's strange verbal warning, articulately and firmly spoken, seeped into my subconscious, his voice raspy with steely gravitas. The face was peeled away from the car and led away by the police, the face still turned towards me. The images of the man's pitted face and shaven head seared itself into my memory as his words continued to ring through my head. My mother tutted and muttered, Louisa breathed heavily and disapprovingly- something I am sure she had learned from her parents- but secretly I was thrilled and desperate to know more. As the car pulled away, I braved to ask "What is all that about Mum?"

"They're just people with nothing better than to do than to protest." She was curt with her reply.

"About what Mum?"

"Just things you wouldn't understand."

It was now clear that my mother had no wish to proceed with this line of conversation and that bugged me. I was rattled by her reluctance to explain what she clearly knew was going on and I resented my mother for making me feel like this. Why wouldn't I understand? I was 15; school had briefed us on the subject of safe sex, what more was there to know? Life began with sex. It was simple but it was adults who complicated everything. Sadly and irritatingly my mother didn't see it like that, despite my irate protestations. I guess that that was her job; to protect and serve. So I shrank back into my seat, inwardly bemused at the hypocrisy of my expensive education. Slowly, I came round; stumbled back into reality. Louisa was still nattering on blindly with her inane bubble of meaningless, childish gossip about homework, lip gloss and girls from school, a word of which I hadn't really taken in as I had been so focussed on the peephole to the adult world that I had just been shown. The car lurched to a halt again, but on this occasion we got out and stalked across the car park, our prey at the foreground of our minds and all else put to one side.

It had only just struck me that we hadn't gone into the centre of town as I had expected- and arrogantly boasted to my father. Conversely, we had driven in the opposite direction to the outlet village just outside town. It was a huge collection of shops; a self-contained centre with everything for the dedicated shopper. It was something which I should have been excited about, ecstatic, perhaps but at the least enthusiastic. At the bottom of the pit, in my soul, I knew the reality. It was a discount centre, a league to which last season's clothes were relegated, and demoted to a division where clothes were slung onto racks as if they were sheep on the slaughter man's wagon. Boxes of reductions heaped in the aisles like coal slag in the valleys and blaring red signs boldly and promiscuously offering their wares. I felt cheap and cheated. This wasn't what my mother had promised but the argument between my parents had been a foreboding sign, had I not been so submerged in my own desires to read it.

Rain clouds began to shed their angry load as we crossed the car park. It was dark and the air smelt heavy with the prospect of a storm. As we reached the shelter of the centre, the spattering of water globules started to hit the ground with the popping sound that kernels of grain make in the frying pan. As the doors closed protectively around us the spray decorated the sparkling glass. My mother continued to stride towards the shops; a ship heading for port after a long, difficult, voyage. She was determined, dragging everything in her wake with her. We were seagulls following the trawler.

To that point it seemed the longest day of my short life, although since then there have been others much worse. That day, my mother and I were destined to disagree on everything. Perhaps it was as a result of the stabbing irritation that reminded me of the treachery of my mother, which taunted me and goaded me into being deliberately rebellious. We started at one end of the mall and went into every shop until we got to the end. There was a clear pattern to the war I raged on my mother. My mother would meander through the racks and mannequins, eyeing different pieces here and there. I would trail behind, lazy with my gait, destructively grating the toes of my shoes against the polished floor, my eyes scanning the racks quickly for the most daring, controversial, provocative and frequently (and not coincidentally) the most expensive dress, skirt or top. Without variation my mother's indignation would be eventually provoked into a scorching fury.

"I really don't think that is appropriate, darling. What about this?" She would begin rationally and calmly, perhaps a slight hint of exasperation at the edges of her voice. "This" was from the sale rack. It could have been last season's at best, who knows what at worst. In the bright artificial strip lighting it swung limply and cheaply from the hanger in her hand.

"Don't like it." My short, terse reply cut my mother's next sentence before it was thought and I turned away on my heels.

"Why?" She was still being reasonable.

"It isn't me." I threw the dismissal back over my shoulder.

"Why don't you try it on?" She tried talking to my back.

"Waste of time, I don't like it. Alright?" My voice was heavy on the final word and I dropped my hip, jutted my chin out, going into attack mode.

"What do you want?" Her patience was beginning to wane as she placed a very specific and accusatory emphasis on the "do".

"This." I replied brightly. I presented her with a black, strappy dress in velvet that I could tell would sleekly coat my just post pubescent body. It would be a dead cert to get some testosterone flowing. My mother's eyes flashed at me. It was obvious that a similar image had forced itself into my mother's mind, provoking an entirely different reaction. In deliberate staccato monotones she said, "I will not buy that for you."

"Why?" I turned the tables. I wanted to hear her struggle to answer the question. But she didn't.

"Because I will not have you going to that social dressed up like some eighteen year old slut." I was impressed at my mother's eloquence whilst going nuclear. She had shocked me into silence. I held up a dazzling red micro skirt in my left hand as a purportedly reasonable alternative.

"What about this?" I said weakly. Her eyebrows arched towards the ceiling so high they almost reached a point whilst her vivid green eyes maintained a fearless contact with me. I didn't dare persist. I had lost the battle.

We went round the mall three times by the end of our trip and my mother and I had countless number of "incidents" in various outlets. Many often resulted in my storming from the shop, screaming at my mother, at which point she would laugh and calmly walk away, her look of absolute disgust at whatever provocative article I had selected settled the spat. A compromise was eventually reached under which I was bought a pair of black patent sling back shoes with an inch and a half heel, a short black skirt which flared out slightly at the hem and was made of a shiny material to be worked with a black sleeveless top with a slash neck. No slinky black dress but I felt the skirt would be short enough for people to notice me. As an additional sweetener, my mother had promised me to do my hair and makeup. Finally, a truce was called.

My mother had no rein over Louisa who had been given cash by her father to "get something pretty". Her assigned colour had been pink and she had found a pink dress, short, but with a full skirt that bounced when she walked. It had no sleeves but had a v-neck and thin slender shoulder straps. She looked beautiful, almost like a ballerina. I didn't want to concede that to her but I, with seemingly good grace, admitted she looked good, turning to hide my green rage, the seeds of which the arguments with my mother had sewn in the pit of my stomach.

Louisa giggled all the way back to the car. "Do you really think these shoes will be okay?" She asked me. I nodded, non-committedly, although I desperately wanted to tell her that the delicately elegant satin sandals would look awful, but I couldn't because it wasn't true and to say so would be nothing but a jealous lie, solely and selfishly designed to make me feel better.
"What about the bag?" Louisa had bought a pretty bag which matched her dress really well. "You can put your things in it on Friday too, if you like." She offered sincerely, knowing that I hadn't been able to negotiate a bag in the deal.
"Thanks, that'll be great. Do you want to come round to mine to get ready, after school on Friday?" I countered, seething with rage because my mother had steadfastly refused to buy a bag as well as the shoes so that I had been forced to choose between the two. Still I felt humiliated and embarrassed in

front of Louisa. My mother had ignored my defiant statements and threats and had walked away, apparently ignoring me with ease.

"Yes, great, I'll ask my mother when I get home". Louisa was always enthusiastic.

"Mum!" I yelled lazily at my mother, whilst trailing behind her by some yards. "It's alright for Louisa to come round to get ready after school on Friday isn't?" I yelled loudly across the lobby of the mall, in which my obnoxious shouts echoed and reverberated against the glass. My mother turned slowly, ignoring my goading demands, to stare at me. "Yes," she said very quietly, hushed and almost in a whisper, I turned immediately to Louisa.

"Mum says yes," I sang out and swung my bags of new clothes carelessly so that the bottoms of the thin plastic bags glanced along the shiny floor of the mall. My mother turned and said that we were going. "But you haven't bought anything for yourself, Mum!" I called with cruel insincerity.

"I don't need anything, let's get going home. Louisa's mum will be wondering where we are." And with that we set off for the car.

Chapter 4

That week, the school hours passed by at an excruciatingly slow pace; time can be so cruel and painful when you're

39

looking towards the future, however far down that road you are peering. The work was boring and dull, which wasn't unusual. The teachers made sure we couldn't discuss the social and my parents continued their argument. They snapped at each other like hungry old crocodiles, snarling over the breakfast table, which had become a sort of barricade. My father looked grey, his features withered and his shoulders slumped, in a stark contrast to my mother, she was direct and upright, stomping around the house, slamming whatever was at hand and muttering her insults and her angry, rude thoughts quietly but clearly audible. On hearing particularly rude comments, my father would eventually retaliate and turn on her.

"When are you going to let this drop? It wasn't my fault, I checked and I told them about it. The client ignored me. I'll show you the file if you like!"
"You didn't try hard enough!" was my mother's terse retort before a frost bitten silence descended upon the house because neither me nor my father felt sufficiently brave to speak, we kept our heads below the parapet to avoid my mother's blasts of rage and fury. Finally, on Friday morning, I summoned the strength to speak to her.
"Um, err, Mum, have you remembered that Louisa is coming home from school with me tonight?" I approached her tentatively, unsure if I'd yet been forgiven for my part in the

fight.

"Of course." My mother released a loud sigh.

"You must be looking forward to tonight." My father ventured to comment, hoping to create some conversation.

"Yeah, absolutely, everyone's been talking about it all week. You know, who's wearing what, who's going to whose house to get ready, we've agreed all our schemes you know, that's why I'm wearing black." I chattered merrily to dad, trying to divert the attention from any possible further conflict.

"What time does it start?"

"7pm and I think it finishes at 10.30pm. There's a proper disco and everything."

"Sounds great. I'll be there to pick you up or is Louisa's mother bringing you back?"

"Oh! I don't know!" I stole a panicked glance at my mother.

"Louisa's mother is picking you up." She interjected sharply and pointedly.

"Right-o. As long as you are sorted." Dad conceded.

"You finish your breakfast and get ready. We're leaving in five minutes. I don't want you to be late." My mother hurried me along. I duly obeyed, as I wasn't prepared to risk engaging her wrath so early in the day, I swallowed the last mouthful of cereal and sprinted upstairs to get my stuff for school.

By the time I got back downstairs, my mother was in the Range Rover with her hand on the horn, blasting noises, screaming for me to hurry. My father kissed me goodbye with an exasperated intake of breath and waved as we backed out of the drive, I had the feeling he was wishing me luck.

The school day crawled along and eventually finished. At half past 3, Louisa and I piled out of the front door with everyone else as we all yelled our goodbyes and see-you-laters. A buzz hovered over us all, a swarm of anticipation, chatter and excitement. Louisa and I dived into the back of the car and sprawled across the seat as mum fought her way through the battlefield that was the parade of mothers' vehicles picking up their young ladies from school. We meticulously planned our preparations for the evening ahead.

We didn't notice the journey home; we were really excited about the prospect of the social, the disco and meeting the boys from St. Augustine's. It was the local catholic boy's school, which was very highly regarded, rather exclusive and very expensive.

"Did you hear Miss Smith tell Olivia that the St Augustine's boys were from very wealthy families and even at fifteen, our introduction to them could be extremely advantageous to us?" Louise informed us. She went to tell us that in the locality, the boys from St. Augustine's generally went on to become doctors, lawyers, stockbrokers and accountants. They would already be good rugby players, cricketers or rowers. St. Augustine's had a famous chapel choir and all of the boys had to sing in the choir during their first year. Depending on their first year, the boys were then directed either towards music or sport and Louisa and I had differing view on prospective suitors.

"I see a balcony, where my Romeo will sing arias and lullabies up to me as I listen from my boudoir." Louise spoke dreamily.

I, on the other hand, imagined a strong, athletic, rugby man who would save me from some sort of situation, whisking me away to safety into his comforting arms. I didn't dare reveal to Louisa or anyone else my romantic day dreams that occurred on an increasingly frequent basis in the build up to the social. I couldn't face that much ridicule. My nerves tingled with excitement, I wanted to shout and shake my arms to expel the nervous energy. However, it would not do for Louisa to see me act like a mad person, so I quickly restrained these urges.

My mother had barely stopped the Range Rover before Louisa and I bounded out of the car and scrambled into the house, shoes, coats and school bags discarded as they flew into the study to the left of the front door. I yelled a cursory "hello" to my father who acknowledged my greeting with a grunt as Louisa and I raced each other to my bedroom, doing a very accurate impression of a stampeded of elephants.

My bedroom was what many people, I suppose, might call a suite. It had an en-suite bathroom and an extensive cupboard that could be described as a "dressing room". Aware of the importance of the evening and the preparation that it would require my mother had been into my room and had put everything back into its place. (I don't think I appreciate that care and consideration at the time.) Quite often for me that place had been the floor, but my mother had seen it put right. Louisa and I yelled, screamed and jumped around the room for a minute, danced around the floor before falling backwards and breathless onto my bed. What would we do first?

"Right. You're the guest, you go in the shower first." I offered.
"Cool. Shall I use this towel?" Louisa picked up the thick fluffy white towel that had bounced off the bed when we had fallen on to it and which I knew would have a soft fragrance of sunshine as mum had done the laundry that day.
"Yeah, I think Mum left that one for you."
"Great," she rummaged through her rucksack and dug out her wash things. She disappeared into the en-suite.

The room was then eerily quiet, something was missing. Music. Something to get us in the mood was required, as if we could have too much of a good thing. I flicked through my CD's. Only now upon reflection, that simple act seems so wrong. Someone once told me that once upon a time the music industry was unregulated, that it was a huge industry with many varied groups of singers, bands of musicians and solo artists who sang and played all sorts of music; soul, popular music and rock. Apparently at that time, in most parts of the World, they were completely uncensored and the lyrics were often political calls to arms. I didn't recognise any of these styles and I had had to be played samples before I would believe it.

Eventually, the desired aging effect worked with brilliant subtlety. Dad got the camera and snapped us posing in the garden, underneath the ancient crippled apple tree, that slanted on an absurdly acute angle. Its fruit is just beginning to take a recognisable form, unlike the young girl in the black, appearing to be already old before her time, standing to the right in the now decrepit photograph.

This battered photograph is secretly stored in my wallet. I dare not take it out for fear of the social worker seeing me and reporting me to the doctor. I am supposed to start afresh with no memory of the past, as a piece of plasticine that can be moulded into the future. I know that the dappled sunlight filtering through the leaves of the apple tree will have faded and the edges have been eaten away by time, but the knowledge that the photograph escaped the attempted purge of my soul has nurtured a small intense flame flickering at the bottom of my heart.

The school hall was joyously and festively decorated with balloons, netting, ribbons and sheets, which failed to conceal the fact that eleven hours previously, we had all been crammed together, sitting impatiently whilst hearing readings and lectures in Friday assembly. BMW's, Jaguars, Mercedes and Porsches stopped briefly to drop their precious cargo's at the door, before departing with waves, shouts, and more often than not a flashy wheel spin and a tremulous roar of the engine. As our modern day carriage approached the door and slowly came to a halt on the yellow gravel, we could see boys hanging around, awkward in their tailored jackets and ties. Ties, which now I think about it, were probably handed down through their families, three or four times over, invariably striped with blue, green, red and even pink. Some had emblems of various clubs, and others just looked too big making us giggle. But they still managed to stroll, not quite carefreely, into the hall, pushing, shoving, laughing and shouting with a pearlescent blend of anticipation, anxiety and arrogance. We floated into the alluring darkness and musty warmth of the hall; the dry ice scented the hall with a sweet, smoky odour creating an enigmatic atmosphere in which to hide. The boys assembled around the door, in groups, ignoring the girls as they trooped through for the first trip to the toilet of the evening. Communal visits to the bathroom on the half hour, every half hour were not my thing, as far as I was concerned they were simply just opportunities to stalk the channel between the two groups of boys who would ignore the impatient and haughty attempts of the girls to catch their eyes.

Louisa and I met up with the others after peering for a moment through the dark, foggy, forest of bodies. We grabbed some colourful but disappointingly harmless cocktails, although I remember the sugar and e-numbered additives probably had a worse effect but without the hangover. As we had seen in films and on television, we held our glasses with what we deemed to be elegance and grace. All of us were fairly proficient at ballet and although we were all aware that none of us were going to take it any further, like all the other girls we were itching for an opportunity to display our dancing skills to everyone else.

Finally it started. The music had been pumping for a while but no-one had dared to break the empty dance floor by themselves. Now a large group of girls, from a different class had stepped out of the conglomerate that clung to the walls of the hall, taking a chance on surviving any ridicule to start waving their bodies in time to the music. Their defiance launched an exodus of girls from the shadows into the dazzling, dancing lights of the disco. Sophia grabbed my hand, I caught Louisa, who dragged someone else and we established our space on the dance floor. Our ballet classes had taught us moves that were useful; we writhed, bounced, wriggled and pranced around the dance floor, generally looking quite silly but thinking we were significantly cooler than everyone else. We took a break to catch our breath, and drink in some of the sweet juices of our cocktails, when I caught my first glance of Philip.

Philip. The first step on my road to self discovery and then ultimately my self destruction.

Philip was gorgeous; blond, tanned with eyes as dark as roasted chestnuts. I caught a glimpse of him in the newspaper yesterday. The past fifteen years seem to have done little to him; a few wrinkles to the corners of his eyes, slightly softer jowls and his hair thinning a little towards the front. He had been promoting some new policy in his role as Surgeon General. A smart blonde lady stood proudly erect at his side, it took me a moment to recognise the toned, tanned frame clothed in a beautifully tailored red suit as that of my old friend, Louisa. My stomach turned with the hateful acid that my returning memories disturbed, knowing that they wouldn't give me the time of day now, and not just because they wouldn't recognise me.

Back then though his smile was broad and sincerely

generous, as he leaned casually against the climbing rails, surveying everything before him. I felt my chest constrict and I took a sharp inhalation, he was beautiful. His shoulders were powerful but his left hand was marked with a dark birth mark that stretched from his wrist to the tip of his small finger. He kept pushing his sand coloured hair back with his left hand. It was a glimpse that seemed to last forever and I then spent the next half an hour, stealing glances at him whilst talking to the girls. I managed to put him out of my mind when we returned to the dance floor but the tempo of the evening suddenly switched to a softer, slower pace for which I was entirely unprepared, almost disappointed. I started to make my way back to my drink with the others, but as I turned I came face to face with Philip, almost bumping into him.

"Dance with me?" he enquired casually, leaning towards me.
"Yes, that'd be nice." I admitted and submitted to his hand as he led me back onto the dance floor. There was something strange about the way in which my stomach formed a tight ball, contracting and relaxing every now again through this slow mellow piece of music, despite everything else that happened later, I have never been so nervous in my life.

I've heard it said that when we're old, reflecting on our lives past, we learn to recognise certain moments in our lives to which we are able to attach such significance that they can be referred to as "defining". An elderly lady named Betty, once told me that these moments are what make us who we are, make our lives what they are; choices. Like the maze at Hampton Court, we all come out in the end but by which way and how long it takes us, no-one can tell. This was the first fork in my maze.

We stepped into each other, I placed my arms under his, he took my left hand and my right settled into the small of his back, my head fell gently on to his chest. We began to sway together, slowly turning in a circle. I was unable to tell whether the light headed feeling I had was due to the circling motion or his close presence.
"I'm Philip by the way." His chocolaty voice was clear over the music.
"Fenn. Nice to meet you."
"Nice to meet you too, you're from St. Cats?"
"Yes, don't like it much, far too strict, You're from St. Augustine's?" I tried not to sound overly impressed.
"Yup, hoping to stay on for A-levels and then to Uni and military college."
"Sounds like you know what you want then."
"Well, I want to be a doctor in the Army. Dad's in the Army and my mother is a doctor. What about you?"
I realised with a cold rush that I had spent the last fifteen years of my life, messing around. I didn't have a clue, all I knew was

that I loved using and studying words.

"I'm not sure yet," I stuttered, dreading the moment, when he no longer found me interesting. "I like writing, so I guess teaching or literature college or something like that might be fun. " I retrieved my senses from the bottom of my stomach.

"Sounds like the beginning of a plan to me." he teased.

"I suppose so. It will do for now." I giggled and he rolled his eyes upwards. The song had changed but the mood hadn't. The forest had retreated back to the walls as the individual bodies became couples and solitary lurkers loitered around the edges, jealously eying those who had bagged a chance.

Betty later told me that such isolation hurts human beings; rejection is always keenly felt like an icy north wind in early January. I could see it then, although I didn't recognise the ugly emotion etched on their faces despite their best efforts to conceal these woes of teenage angst. I felt a warm glow of smug, self satisfaction that I had been picked, not left at the edge to feel desolate and unwelcome, discarded and second best. I smiled to myself and suddenly felt Philip's head bend towards me, his broad smile reaching out to me, I smelt what I presumed was his father's aftershave, as his freshly shaved cheek, brushed mine, his lips searching for that first kiss. My heart leapt into my throat as I succumbed like any other fifteen year old girl would to a gorgeous sixteen year old boy on the cusp of manhood. I desperately wanted us to remain like that-lips pressed tight together- for eternity, I can't say how long it lasted but suddenly the music stopped, the harsh strip lighting of the school hall flooded the room and Louisa was casually coughing behind me.

Philip and I exchanged lustful longing looks as Louisa dragged me to her mother's car.
"I can't believe it," Louisa squealed and squeezed my arm as we flopped onto the back seat of the car, weary from all the excitement.
"What?" I murmured obliviously.
"You and Philip Sanderson. He's like the catch of the century."
"Really?" I gazed blissfully happily out of the window into the summer darkness.
"You know his father is a commanding officer, really high up in the Army and his mother is the doctor who advises the President. They're really quite a rich family you know. Oh! And I hear that he is a really fab rugby player. Imagine those muscles! Did you get to feel them?" Louisa carried on twittering away ignorant of my increasing discomfort in front of her mother as I came-to from my reverie.
"I dunno."
"You are going to see him again, aren't you?" Louisa demanded, looking straight at the side of my face.
"I um…didn't get his telephone number." A cold numbness fell over me. What a disaster, the best looking guy at the social.

Perhaps he didn't want my number, perhaps he didn't want to speak to me again, or perhaps he had just used me. Deflation set in and Louisa conspicuously fell silent.

"What about you?" I ventured.

"Oh I danced with this boy called Peter, but that's all. No kissing, not like some I can mention!" and she winked at me. I watched the faintest trace of disapproval flicker across Louisa's mother's face in the rear view mirror and then disappear. She had me marked down as "one of those girls" now. She'd probably not want Louisa to be my friend anymore but thankfully Louisa had now moved on to safer ground.

"Did you see what Kate Martin was wearing? I think I saw it in that cheap shop on Broad Street. It was awful, like something my sister would wear. She didn't look as good as you which is why she didn't get to kiss Philip Sanderson! He!he!" Once more, we were back into the quagmire of my reputation.

Chapter 5

The sun is shifting in the garden; the patterns in the dapples of light are merging into the shadows of the garden shed as mid afternoon passes. I dare not stop to believe that all that has happened; many will not believe my history and will put my seemingly paranoid nonsense down to the fact I read books and attribute my scare mongering lies to the influence of cinema. A pale pink rose bends its head in deference to the boisterous breeze that is gusting through the garden, the leaves of the rose scratch against the protective window pane that is dotted sporadically with droplets of water forced from the foreclosing and foreboding rain clouds which begin to extend their tendrils of gloom across the kitchen. But the rose does not yield- its petals remain steadfast.

I do not see her rise from the chair and wander around the table behind me. The pain takes me by surprise; a sharp stab in my shoulder followed by an immediate dull ache immediately, the memory and guilt arising phoenix like to verify my humanity. As the pain ebbs away, anger emerges from the depths and I struggle to focus through the darkening red mist that has descended to surround me. I press my eyelids together, squeezing the kitchen out of my vision, inhaling slowly to take in the homely fragrances of the kitchen and then I release my fingers from the fixed grasp of my fist, permitting the red mist to dissipate harmlessly while the social worker faces the kettle, her back shielding me from her view. The mug of tea steams furiously as she places it firmly in front of me, the bang against the pine almost audible. Her eyes dare not leave my now placid face.

We went to see the film; a carefully written piece about a policeman in a murder investigation who realises, too late as it turns out, that his destiny means he will be the accused in the same investigation. The dialogue was so pointedly correct that Someone had Reviewed it, whether changes had been imposed on the writer, it was difficult to tell. It was fun nevertheless and I was all set to leave the warmth of the crowded amphitheatre as the final credits began to roll down the screen, but a flash of confusion streaked across Philip's face, returned and became a grimace. "That's my brother's name" he murmured. "Stanley. Z. Sanderson. It must be him. He's listed as a script writer." Philip was stunned, we both knew the treatment to which writers could be subjected by the President and the risk such an occupation held. Confusion was now replaced by concern and consternation.

"I didn't know. I had no idea. Mum and Dad'll freak. They thought that his talk of writing was just that, that's why they let him work at Alfred's place. What the hell are they going to do? What should I tell them?" His voice began to crack. The enormity of the moment struck me, a bell tolling inside my chest his parents were closely linked to the President. How would they deal with any embarrassment? But we didn't know what precisely was going on and therefore Philip needed to speak to Stanley. I told him so.

"I know. Let's go. I don't know if he's home," Philip seemed perplexed, unsure, almost disorientated. I nodded my head, not knowing the right thing to say as we headed in silence from the cinema and back towards the bus stop where Philip kissed me on the cheek almost absent-mindedly and said in earnest that he would phone me. I watched him walk slowly heel through to toe, head down, hands deep in his pockets. His shoulders were rolled forward as he became an increasingly forlorn figure as the bus rolled me away from him.

True to his word, Philip phoned me the next evening. Whether it was because he liked me or because I was the only he could talk to about Stanley, I didn't know, but it didn't really worry me because I was sincerely glad I was needed to help. He hadn't found Stanley; his flat had been empty by the time Philip had got there half an hour after he had left me at the bus stop. Alfred had told him that he hadn't heard from Stanley since he had left his job earlier in the week, apologising to Alfred but refusing to explain why or where he was going. A vulnerability gilded the edge of Philip's voice to which I couldn't help but warm, however the cold reality that I could not avoid was that Philip would have to tell his parents. How could he not tell them that their eldest son was a writer and had now gone missing? It was a truth that Philip accepted with reluctance as heavy as a drunk waking from his alcoholically induced slumber. I could hear the weight drag in this voice; his words interrupted by long pauses, an inability to finish sentences emerged. We didn't talk about anything else although we talked for an hour. I explained hurriedly that I had to go when my father started to complain about the length of time that I'd been on the telephone, shouting loudly and crudely at me,

56

asking who was paying for the phone call. As I said goodbye to Philip the rage boiled behind my eyes and the pit of my stomach was burning furiously. My father had been so insensitive, so rude and so very impolite. I didn't stop to acknowledge the fact that my father had no idea about the emotionally charged yet fragile conversation he had so brutally intruded upon with such angry force. Dropping the phone receiver on to its cradle seemed to open some sort of gateway into that rage. White hot fury surged through me.

"How could you be so rude?" I demanded loudly, striding into the kitchen and slamming the kitchen door so hard that is bounced against the cupboard behind it. "You didn't need to ask me who was paying for it while I was still speaking to Philip."

"Yes. I did." My father retorted sharply. "You need to realise the value of money."

"But you didn't need to do it whilst I was on the phone to Philip!" I protested.

"It seemed like the most appropriate time to do it. You don't know what things cost. Have you seen the latest phone bill? No. And that jacket you're wearing, do you know what proportion of our weekly income it represents?"

"What's that got to do with you being rude and thoughtless about anyone else?!!"

My father took a sharp intake of breath and exhaled heavily, blowing the expelled air into an imaginary balloon.

57

"And since when did we get so obsessed with money, anyway? You're such a bloody accountant!" I screamed at him, the humiliation of Philip having heard my father quibble about pennies, burning within me.

A sharp screech of the doorbell suspended my verbal assault upon my father. As my mother drew back the door, a wide burly shaven-headed man filled the door step, casting a wide shadow through the doorframe.

"Mrs Smythe?" He demanded politely.
"Yes? Can I help you?"
"I am sorry, but…. I've come to collect the Range Rover." His appearance may have been rough but his voice and demeanour were gentle, his shoulders rolled forward as he tried to make himself seem smaller. . It would have been obvious that my mother was not going to be a problem, although the stammer came back in an instant.
"Uh, uh, I…..I….. I'm sorry, I'm not sure that I heard you correctly?" She flicked her head to refer the man to her husband. My father's head bowed low.
"I'm here to take the Range Rover away."
"Oh you mean to the garage?"
"No, the repayments haven't been made for the last six months. Apparently someone at the office spoke to your husband last week." He tried to helpfully remind her, and then

looked past her to my father.

My mother turned to my father, who was slumped at the kitchen table, head resting on his forearms. His chest was heaving heavily.

"Y-y-y-you knew about this?" She turned on my father, shaking her head slightly, eyes pleading with him to say that it wasn't true. My father may not have volunteered the truth, but it seemed that he couldn't lie directly to my mother's face. He slowly raised his face, eyes red and clouded, and his bottom lip struggling to maintain control. He nodded with a sad, pathetic resignation, and suddenly I saw the years break out of my father and cling to the folds of his skin, and seep into the crevices of his wrinkles. I should have felt sorry for him, I should have been shocked at the sight of my father and I should have been selfishly worried about how much time I might have left with him. I didn't. Any sympathy I might have had was swamped and swallowed by the rage that had bitterly and stubbornly remained and had been re-ignited by the realisation that we were about to lose everything, very slowly, to be deprived of everything item by item and to be subjected to the most pathetic and humiliating public flogging.

There was a horrible stifling pause. My mother simply stared at my father, I glared violently at him while the Bailiff simply glanced at all three of us.

"I have the paperwork. It's quite new, we'll still get a good price for it, and so if you would sign just here, the boss says you shouldn't hear from us again."

My mother meekly nodded, running a fearful hand that was taut with tension and nerves, through her now quickly greying hair. She gently took the pen and quickly signed at the requested place. She turned hurriedly, looking towards the floor, arms wrapped around her own waist protectively. A quiet, small cough came from the doorway.

"Mrs Smythe, could I have the keys please?"
My mother's head snapped back in alarm, but she acquiesced quietly. She bit her lip continuously, eyes searching for safety but not knowing where to look. Silently she gathered the keys from the telephone table and handed them over. The Bailiff bowed his head quickly, muttered an almost inaudible "thanks", before efficiently and professionally getting into the Range Rover and driving off.

You know we never did hear from them again. I expect that they were as embarrassed as we were, especially later when they realised what had happened like almost everyone did from - what were actually wildly accurate- stories in the Press.

My mother watched the fading rear lights of the Range Rover leaving the drive and pushed the door closed. She looked briefly at my father, a glance full of sorrow as she dejectedly climbed the stairs, creaking under both their burdens.

The respite for my father from my brutal onslaught was brief and ended as suddenly as it had started.

"So my phone calls are to be monitored? They've taken mum's car? What next? Stopping my pocket money? Sending me to Mill Grove High? This is fucking crap." I spat my words onto the crumpled heap on the table that was my father. For a moment I looked through the kitchen window and out into the garden.

"Where's the boat?" I demanded combatively. "Oh I see! They took that as well." I sneered. "Oh let's see what else they've taken!" and I stormed into the lounge.

"What a fucking surprise, they've already taken the television, oh, and the stereo." The walls were bereft of the treasured oil paintings my parents had collected before I was born. I continued to shout and stamp, pounding the wooden floor boards, slamming doors tempestuously. I eventually raged back into the kitchen. My father hadn't moved. His docility now began to irk me, offending my sense of righteous indignation; he wasn't fighting to explain himself, he wanted to just let me blow myself out. Scant hope.

"Don't you care what you've done? You're wrecking my life. How can I go to school on Monday? I mean what's mum going to drive?"

And then finally, my father's sorrow laden head began to rise out of its shell, his aged neck straining with its burden, as his eyes withdrew with fear, but continued to creep up to meet my volatile, challenging glare.

"You're not going back to St. Catherine's." He conceded quietly, in a withering, shrinking voice, a truth that I had dismissed as soon as I had said it earlier.

"Liar!!" I screamed at him.

I quickly became smothered by the tense smoggy atmosphere that enveloped the room; I felt my heart beat like a howitzer gun against my tightening rib cage. My brain was screaming for air, sense and space. The early evening light advanced across the kitchen, throwing just another ingredient into an already bubbling cauldron. The house was still and quiet. No sound from my mother upstairs, there was an uneasy and wretchedly fragile calmness after the battle as my father and I surveyed the casualties. After a moment of frozen silence, the anger and poisonous disappointment ripped through my torso and exploded out of me through my throat into a voice of which I had no recognition. It was quiet and small, but echoed against the harsh, hard barrier between my father and me.

With every emotion and feeling behind it, I said, "You've betrayed me dad. I feel let down. You were supposed to provide for me and keep me safe. How can I feel safe when you've failed to do that? Strangers walking in here and taking stuff. What's the point of you being here?"

And then I screamed. "I just wish you were dead!"

And I turned and fled, through the front door which slammed behind me, any words that my father might have cried were cut off from me. I just kept going, blindly but instinctively sprinting straight across the road. I stretched out to reach the other side of the road safely and briefly glanced behind me. I caught sight of my father chasing me, running towards the road, shouting for me, urgently pleading for me to stop and come back. Hatred surged through me, I wanted him to hurt like I was, as I looked at my father, I turned back to ignore him, to keep running. It was the last time I saw him.

Chapter 6

I didn't need anyone to confirm it. I knew he was dead. Guilt? Remorse? No, more an epiphany. My first reaction was the recognition that in the final momentary glance behind me, I had seen him stop. As far I as I was concerned, he had slowly and deliberately stepped into the road at the optimum moment. He had chosen to die.

"Are you okay love?" Hands reached out to me.

"She saw the whole thing, bless her." I shrugged the snaking arms away from me.

"What the hell happened?" Faces around me swam in the faint blue lights of the police car.

"The poor man stood no chance." The taxi driver or my father, I wondered.

"Road's a bloody death trap. An accident was bound to happen."

"How is he?" I saw the grim shake of the head. The dark plastic sheet hid my father's body but it could not cover the seeping pool of blood that was creeping across the tarmac road.

During the eons that seemed to have passed since my father's death countless counsellors both at school and hospital have asked me to describe what I felt at this particular point. I have always greeted such questions with scornful disdain, considering myself above such need for close analysis. With complete frankness, I felt nothing; certainly not guilt. Some doctors would shout "she was in shock" so as to account for my cold numb silence and perhaps I was. But at the precise moment at which I realised he had been killed I felt nothing but a strong sense of purpose; he had chosen to die and that that was what he wanted. As things progressed, did I realise and accept that he hadn't thought about it until he chose to do it; the opportunity simply presented itself and he chose to grasp it. But the anger refused to fade- he had chosen to die, to leave my mother and me behind alone with the mess he created. I could never forgive him for his cruel cowardice.

An ambulance arrived, it went. My mother appeared and wantingly helpful hands pushed me to her. I should have fought and run then, but shock gripped me in totality and all I could do was to allow myself to be pushed towards the inevitable tea and sympathy.

A tall solemn policeman confirmed that my father was dead by the brief grimace on his face, his eyes closed for a moment. The taxi driver was wandering up and down the pavement, not knowing where to be, not knowing where not to be, not knowing what would happen- charge, conviction, prison, loss of job or confirmation that it was a tragic accident, but there was nothing practical he could do with the bestowal of understanding and forgiveness by my mother and me. I still empathise with him now as I did then; the fog of the unknown is disorientating, confusing and debilitating. I hope he knows that I never blamed him, despite the allegations made by the Prosecution in Court.

My mother sat on the bottom step of the stairs, her world, however imperfect and troubled, had been utterly shattered. As I was pushed through the door, she ran and grabbed me, wrapping herself around me, her tears dissolving into my hair.

I couldn't reciprocate. I just stood there. Hatred still flooded through me. I couldn't forgive him, he had elected the craven path that left Mum and I to deal with everything. I could feel my mother's sobs wrenching at my shoulders. "It's just shock" the neighbour suggested as an explanation for my lack of tears to my mother as she looked questioningly at me. I stood there, solid, no response to her touch. Did she blame me? "It was a tragic accident" she told me, not knowing what I had seen.

It was a shame that I had to go on to ruin such a good tragedy.

Chapter 7

The house became a stench of misery and despair, woe seeped from the walls. My mother wandered from room to room, breathlessly, shuddering against the freezing mists of bereavement. But those mists didn't keep the wolves at bay for long; my father's estate was barren with nothing to support us. As the implication of this state of affairs began to explain itself, my volatile, simmering hatred for my father burgeoned uncontrollably. I couldn't talk about him or listen to other people's pitiful eulogies of sorrow, regret, his seemingly nice perfection. They didn't know? My head screamed with rage and indignation. And yet the bills kept coming which was a reality my mother needed to face quickly. Since my father's business had become successful she hadn't had to work. It was now not a choice or an option - it was a necessity. But what was she to do? In a previous life, before me and my father, she had been a lawyer but could she still do that?

About a month after my father's pathetic death, life at home was still moribund; school was allowing me to stay until the end of the year, when "arrangements" would be reviewed. I hadn't spoken of my father's death to anyone other than to pay lip service to the offers of condolence and sympathy that were submitted to me. The school counsellor was politely but firmly rebuffed by me. On one occasion I had just arrived home after school, my mother was sat at the kitchen table with a man in an immaculate slate grey suit, sharp in all its angles. His white shirt was crisp and starched, his red tie halting me immediately and his briefcase carefully placed at his side. A tiny sun shaped badge sparkled from his lapel. I could see that the steaming tea was freshly made and the stress of whatever this situation was taking a heavy toll on my mother, hair greyer than ever, hands wringing themselves through her ever weakening tresses.

"Hi darling. This is Mr. Thomas, the bank manager. We're just going through some things. Once we've done, I'll get you something to eat. Why don't you pop upstairs and change while we finish?" She was trying so hard to be calm and in control, it was unnerving after all the weeks of the madness of her grief.

I nodded but suspicions began to run through my already battered mind. Affair? She wouldn't. School? They said that they would review it at the end of the year. And as I climbed the stairs slowly, odd words floated up to meet me.

"Amanda, this can't go on. You can't afford the house. If you don't sell it, we will and I can tell you that there won't be much left. You have to tell Fenn." What was he talking about selling?

"Fenn has known no other house, David. It'll be devastating."

"As devastating as losing her father?" A short pause. "She is now 15, she'll be going to a new school next year. A fresh start for you both."

"Hmmmmm."

"How's the job hunting?"

"I've had three interviews. One offer. One rejection, the other I'm waiting to hear."

"That's not bad, certainly progress that I can take to my boss. What's the offer?"

"The Attorney-General's office. They'll put me on courses to get me up to date. Salary of £80,000."

"Cracking news. Have you taken it?

There was a muffled murmur and shuffling. The words mutated into a series of invisible mimes during a pause of absolute stillness as I searched the air for the faintest sound.

"I do understand, but it's a job with a fantastically good salary. I won't be able to stave off the bank if you don't help yourself."

Another inaudible grunt like sound. Was she crying?

"Think about Fenn. She'd still have to change school but life would not be quite so difficult."

"I suppose." The concession was forming in her mind. "And I suppose there will be some sort of intellectual challenge." The takeover was complete, she was theirs.

"It's still office hours now, they'll take the call." David gently nudged her, coaxing her into a decision. Her soft footsteps tapped on the hard floor, quickly followed by the clicks of a number being dialled and then the briefest of pauses.

"Hello? Dr. Ashton? It's Amanda Smythe, about the job offer? It's still open? Yes, great. Well, I accept." She put her claim to the job to whoever was at the other end of the line heartily, although a slight trace of gut-wrenching resignation ran through her chocolate velvet voice.

"Well, I shall see you a week on Monday at 9.30am. Many thanks."

The wave of relief from the kitchen was almost tangible. A soft ripple, barely audible was released and waved across the house, freeing it from its lethargic slumber, a long held breath finally exhaled.

I laughed at the irony much later when I discovered through various ruses that Mr Thomas worked for a government organisation that owned the bank.

I carefully finished my climb upstairs and changed. Attorney-General? I wasn't really sure what this would entail, so I wandered across to the beautiful leather-bound, but practically new, encyclopaedia that had been left for me in her will by my grandmother. I casually flicked through the pristine pages, the photographs still silky, until I found the relevant entry. As I understood it, my mother was going to work for the President's lawyer. I didn't see anything wrong with that; although the thought that my mother would not be there when I got home from whichever I school I would be attending, seemed alien and disconcerting, but wonderfully exciting as the prospect of such precious unguarded time began to seduce me. Perhaps it might not be all bad.

Shortly after my mother started work the void left in our lives began to fill slowly. Despite the trial of the taxi driver being completed some months previously, we received the Coroner's report; there would be no hearing as it was a tragic accident about which there had been nothing that anyone could have done to avoid it. A blip in time. Surprisingly my mother didn't breakdown into a mass of tearful misery and grief when she read the report, contrary to everything I had expected. I think it must have had something to do with the changes in circumstances; upon receipt of the Coroner's report, the life insurance had paid out quickly, a sum which had paid off the mortgage and meant my mother could just focus on the other creditors resulting from my father's benevolence. I, on the other hand, carried on attending St Catherine's, still unsure of what would happen next year. My friends were condoling, sincere with their sympathy and invited me to dinner at theirs when my mother had to work late, which became more often as time wore on and she realised I didn't need her anymore.

It was on one of these occasions that I was at Louisa's house after school, we were in her room, discussing music, school and general gossip. She started rambling on about the next school year as the end of the current one drew near, about exams and what we wanted to do in life.
"In all honesty Lou, I probably won't be there." Her look at me was of quizzical bewilderment, my tone was passive without offering any comment or opinion on the matter.
"What do you mean?" She urged me to say more.
I was leafing through a magazine with beautiful women draped in bold, vivid colours passing before my eyes, their dazzling gold jewellery flashing around the pages, my attention wavered whilst I envied the models and I responded quickly. "Since my father killed himself, money is tight which is why my mother has gone back to work." A cold patch in my stomach spread, freezing my lungs when I realised what I had said.

"Killed himself? It was an accident." Louisa tried to re-assure me. In the brief silence, during which I tried to collect my thoughts and plot my way out of my blunder, there was a creak at the other side of the door, shadows hovered in the crack of light forcing itself under the door and footsteps moving on the stairs to the second floor of the three storey town house.

"I meant to say "got himself killed". He really should have looked before he crossed the road. It was what he always told me." I tried to sound callous, like I blamed him. Not difficult at the time.

"It must be so awful for you." Cooed Louisa, almost maternally.

"It's getting better slowly. Mother and I are sorting things out."

"That's good. Have you heard from Philip?"

I hadn't since the day of my father's death and it had now been a couple of months. Louisa took my silence as a negative and permission to continue her line of enquiry.

"He's probably heard what happened and didn't want to intrude." Louisa offered sagely.

"True. Should I call him?"

"Why not? No harm in testing the water."

As I resolved to telephone Philip the next afternoon after school, we were called to dinner. Dinner was a strange affair, we had spicy kobi beef and noodles but the atmosphere was chilled, slightly tense, a ghostly presence seemed to wander around us as we sat at the long mahogany table in the narrow dining room of Louisa's ancient house, voices echoing in the open eaves and tapestry hangings over the stone fireplace, waving slightly in the draughts of the flickering fire.

"So how are you Fenn?" Louisa's mum started, an unnerving emphasis placed on the "how".

"I'm fine." I said her with assurance and confidence, looking her straight in the eye and allowing a brief smile to break through. The argument with my dad had hardened my ability to deal with adults.

"And your Mum?"

"She's fine too, seems to be working hard and enjoying her new job too."

"It must have been terrible seeing your dad killed like that, especially after the two of you had fallen out so badly." Clearly my mother hadn't felt the need to keep my argument with my father private. I wonder if she regrets that now.

"I didn't see the impact of the accident; I had just crossed the road when it happened." I coolly replied, deciding honesty was the best way to answer her question. I would have to remember, all the lies and I didn't have faith that I could do that accurately yet.

"Oh. But you still heard it all?"

"I suppose so."

"Why didn't he look? I can't understand it. Your father was such an intelligent and careful man." I suffocated a guttural snort of contempt but tried to appear down cast and ashen faced, upset by implication.

"Gloria, I don't think we need to go over this now. Let Fenn be. Fenn, I'm sorry, we were just so shocked." Louisa's father was a wise and kind-looking man.

I murmured a barely audible "no need" and stuffed an obscenely large piece of kobi into my mouth to avoid further conversation. It took me a while to chew through it which left Louisa to regale her parents with tales from school, and me in an uncomfortable peace. I managed to keep eating at inconvenient moments noting, at the same time, the exchange of accusatory glances and forced stares between Louisa's parents. When the meal was over and my offers to help clean up were rejected, I made my excuses and left hurriedly back to the safety of home.

For the first time in a while, when I got home the next evening, my mother was already there. She wasn't in her suit; she was in jeans and a t-shirt- casual for her.

"Hi" she called brightly as I wearily pushed through the heavy front door with its stained glass.

"I thought we might go out for dinner." I shrugged and nodded. Fine by me. We hadn't been out to eat since before my father's death because we knew that people watching would think it inappropriate. It was now four months since my father's death, for three of which my mother had now been working for the President. Irritation started to creep in to me; what was mourning? Who dictated how you mourn someone and for how long?

A fortnight after my father's funeral, my mother had stopped wearing black, instead preferring a pair of jeans and a scarlet polar-neck sweater when we popped out for some groceries late one evening. A bird-necked crone with a wiry frame and long bony fingers pointed at my mother, whilst she leaned over the frozen food chest.
"Your poor husband". She crowed scornfully at my mother. "Barely dead two weeks and you've already shed your mourning clothes." The accusation pierced the cloud of despair that had blanketed my mother and shielded her from outside influences so much so that she went home and threw out her colourful clothes, retaining a wardrobe of black. I seethed at the arrogant woman who presumed that my father had been worthy of her sympathy.

We walked to the local Chinese restaurant, me having stumbled and spluttered my way through my mother's intense interview of my school day. She was excited, her eyes were bright and lively, darting across my face, I could tell she was going to tell me something.
"I've got a promotion. It'll mean more money."
"Great. More hours?" I responded grumpily, I didn't really

resent her being away but a realistic and normal rebellious teen approach was required to avoid being obvious and any consequential suspicion.

"Not really, about the same. Work until it's done. I do have to swear an oath to the President though. Hopefully, you can also stay at school next year."

"Ok." I was a bit puzzled why the oath bit would be necessary.

"I mean, I'll be working with some classified stuff. I have to prove my loyalty so there's a swearing ceremony next week, I really want you to be there." It was a statement, almost an order, no request, no wish. An inhuman statement. "Of course, you'll have to miss school, but you can spend the day at my office. We'll call it work experience if you like, that should appease Ms Clarke." She seemed to have already headed off the objections from the school, I was well and truly corralled into attending and so nodded, seemingly obediently. Her eyes lit up with delight.

Chapter 8

Circumspection permits me to reflect upon the obvious way in which my situation developed. Like a photograph, the final outcome seems to have been always planned, it was a matter of getting there via various short cuts, detours or diversions. I desperately wanted to avoid watching my mother swear allegiance to an entity that I was starting to question, whose principles confused my ordinary sense of being. I could feign illness, pretend there was something on at school that I couldn't miss, like a test but I knew she would be devastated. And whilst I could always steel myself against the shouting in anger, I was never prepared for her total disappointment with the slow, shaking of the head and pursed lips. Now I also recognise that a tiny part of me thought that if my destiny was going to conflict with the establishment, as it inevitably did, surely I shouldn't spurn a chance to see inside the devil's lair, while I was young enough not to be suspected as any form of threat. The thought thrilled me. So no feigned illness, no pretend test, I toddled along behind my mother obediently, slip streaming directly into trouble.

A week later my mother woke me earlier than usual. Sunshine cruelly streamed through my window, dust particles moving slowly and gathering thickly in its glowing embers. My room was warm and safe, I dragged my head off the pillow to see a breakfast tray with a feast, my shoes polished, black skirt pressed and white blouse starched reflecting an effort to impress that was deliberately being made by my mother.

"When you're done with the tray just jump into the shower, wash your hair too. I'll dry it and do it for you." This was serious and I still wasn't sure that I wanted to do this. I churned my thoughts through my head- Dad, school, Louisa's parents. How much trouble could I get in? I was 15?

With my hair dried and straightened, tights pulling at my knees and my school shoes shining brilliantly, we were ready and leaving in my mother's new corporate BMW, the car that now came with her new job. It was inanimate but I didn't trust it or what it stood for, a dark brooding animal purring on the drive. A foreboding sense of heaviness lined my already leaden stomach; the car heading almost automatically to its destination. The journey was only half an hour yet it dragged on, time lingering obstinately. Suddenly the car couldn't seem to travel fast enough, now I just wanted to get there. When we eventually arrived at some imposing black iron gates my mother turned to me and handed me a small oblong plastic card. I was surprised to see my name and photograph on it.
"It's to get you in. I arranged for it especially." I smiled weakly, was she trying to enlist me?

Behind the heavy gate was a tall dark marble building with black windows that effused an authority and mystery. Building 13. It didn't encourage photographs or questions; tourists seemed not to notice it, but by simply being there it forged my mind with fear, reaching out to the universe with its twisted, tangled receivers and emitting particles that screamed to me with blind panic, silent terror and paralytic apprehension. Only I know the turmoil that was ploughing through my entire body in the moment that I swiped the pass card and followed my mother, I begged that no-one could hear my insides rioting and revolting against me squeezing through my narrowing stomach, my energy ebbing away quickly into the timeless abyss.

The dark marble blanketed the interior of the building too, tiny halogen spot lights peppered the ceiling; deceptive stars in an untrustworthy night sky. The corridor surged forwards, my mother's heels announcing her arrival with every step nearer to the front desk. I made a decision that didn't need to be made; go with it, learn, observe and make the most of it. It hit me with the certainty of an airplane crash that I didn't belong here and any return I might make would be involuntary. The sense of foreboding lifted, releasing me from my paralysis. Coyly I traipsed after my mother who was nodding and raising her hand to anonymous colleagues.

The ladies at reception were polite, immaculately well groomed and kitted out with the latest radio headsets.
"Good morning Mrs Smythe. This must be Fenn, welcome to Building 13, young lady. We hope you enjoy your visit." said the blonde lady with an almost genuine tone.
The red haired lady was efficiently talking into the headset, so quietly she was barely audible. It sounded like the murmur of a gentle breeze through bull rushes but still she smiled briefly at

us as we were waved pass the glittering glass desk.

There were two long corridors either side of the glass desk; we bore left and arrived at some glass lifts in a square hall that didn't seem to have a roof. I peered up into what appeared to be an endless darkness that was punctuated with the interior roof lights of the lifts, simply gliding up and down the wall, allowing me to get my bearings in the murky light. A lift arrived and my mother pressed me into the lift, it was just the two of us.
"A-a-a-are you okay?" She smoothed my hair.
"Mum, I'm fifteen. I'm fine. Don't fuss." I hissed at her, not wanting to be embarrassed.
"Great darling."

We arrived at the 31st floor in a matter of seconds; my mother straightened her jacket and pulled herself tall before smartly stepping out of the lift. Things began to blur; the clicking heels, the dark marble, more halogen lights, ebony doors with silver numbers, 311, 312, 313, 314……… Another glass desk with another pair of impeccably dressed clones tending their switchboards. My mother nodded briefly as the receptionists responded to their headphones and we headed to the left again. At the end of the corridor was a final ebony door that had the number 331 etched upon it in silver.

"Well, this is my office." I gazed around the hallway. Despite the gleaming marble, a bleak sense of isolation seeped around the floor, a slight chill echoed off the walls at the same time.

"Cool. Let's see it then." I tried to be encouraging with a positive smile. She placed a light hand on the silver door handle, pushed down and away in one smooth movement and the heavy door swung open smoothly, silent and effortlessly. A plush red carpet covered the floor, pressed tightly to the skirting boards of ebony. The walls were black marble. The only window provided a view that stretched away and along for miles, creating an omnipotent panorama of the city. A similarly large, expensive plasma television screen watched over the room, hanging on the wall opposite a large heavy ebony desk which was accompanied by a similarly heavy and large, high backed leather chair. The plasma screen flicked through various black and white images of scenes that I did not recognise; they looked like mere ordinary citizens going about their daily business. The various individuals were travelling to work, taking the kids to school, meeting friends in the pub. I stood before the screen absorbed by the stories these scenes might be telling. It clicked that these were real people, people in this city, living and breathing here, but being watched by my mother who was now watching me.

"Well, what do you think?" She asked eagerly.

My horror rendered me speechless.

"Do you spy on people mum?"

"No, other people do that for me. These are just the really dangerous people. Look, here." She pointed to a small domed object on her desk. It was black, unassuming and made of heavy plastic. My mother ran her fingers over the dome which began to vibrate quietly, Sounds began to emerge and I could see and hear that they were the sounds to the pictures. She now had audio for her private entertainment show.

"What do you mean by dangerous Mum?" I couldn't fully appreciate just how open she had been, as if there as nothing at all wrong with what was happening.

"Well we think that they pose a danger to the Country."

"How?"

"To the Government."

"What sort of danger?"

"We think that they are participating in and perpetuating rumours and gossip that are contrary to the Government's policies and principles." The words, like a slogan, slid slickly off my mother's tongue, so well-rehearsed.

"So what do you do?"

"I decide if they've done anything wrong."

"Are these people watched all the time?"

"Pretty much."

"And they don't know you're watching them?"

"No."

"Have you been watching me?"

"It would be a matter of protection with you rather than for any criminal justice purpose." Her words came with such an earnest belief that I don't think she ever felt that this was wrong; from here it now seems the brainwashing must have been complete long before this.

"So have you been watching me?" I insisted. A nausea rose within me, a foul taste coating my mouth and I tried to hide my disgust.

"Yes."

"Personally or do you get some perverted nerd with a computer obsession to do to it?" I spat my words at her.

"I'm not going to dignify that with an answer. I've told you that it's for your own safety. You don't have to believe me, but I'd like you to trust me on that."

"So how do you decide if someone has done something that, how did it go? *Is contrary to the Government's policies and principles*?""

"You have to understand that the President is looking after you all, protecting you and keeping you from harm. Does it matter how he does it?"

"I remember something in history about electoral mandates. Seeing as there hasn't been a free vote for years, his must have expired by now?"

I had accidentally set off the trap. My mother's eyes flashed between me and the door. Her brow furrowed deeply, her face knitted with fear.

"So what time is your ceremony?" I tried to recover the situation.

"12pm. So we've got quite a bit of time. Let me give you a couple of files to read while I check my emails, voicemails and post. Then I'll show you around."

I nodded with meek submission. I had overstepped the mark, realising that I had inadvertently put both of us in a precarious position. I could hear my mother's thoughts praying that no-one had heard me.

She thrust at me a pile of documents, made up of nine red folders, each of which was about four inches thick. Six men, three women. All under the age of 40, two professors, six graduates and a playwright.

He was on the top.

His photograph.

A thousand voices erupted in my head. The loudest of all amongst the deafening cacophony was Philip's. My mother was focussed on her computer and I guessed that she hadn't noticed my reaction. To be sure I spread the files over the floor, faced down and swapped them around, pushing the red cardboard envelopes over the deep plush, red carpet. I hummed while I worked, sitting cross-legged, leaning against the black leather sofa.

"Fenn, what on earth are you doing?" She almost laughed at me.

"I couldn't work out which one to start with; this was the easiest way to choose." I played along, childlike in my reasoning.

"Fair enough." She shrugged and returned to whatever email was attracting her attention.

I picked the nearest file to me. One I hadn't actually moved because I knew exactly to whom this file related. Blood pumped through and around my body almost inducing in myself a searing uncontrollable panic, as I opened the file in silent terror.

"Stanley Walter Sanderson. British. Male. Former address: 12 Arndale Way, Foxton. School: St. Augustine's. Employment: Not Known. Family: Mother, Father, Younger Brother. Whereabouts: Unaccounted. Last Known Location: London. Charges: Unauthorised film script, defamatory remarks about Government, unauthorised publications, possession of unlawful printed material and membership of an unauthorised group."

I felt like I had run headlong into a brick wall only to bounce off flat onto my back, leaving me staring at the blank empty sky. It took me a moment or two to realise I was still upright when the next question hit me. What should I do? My presence here was on the basis that my mother worked for the President and that she had vouched to those that needed such assurance that I was trustworthy. It was bad enough that I wasn't buying into this crap, but it would be even worse when she found out that I betrayed her trust by disclosing any information I had gained as I felt I must. I could not escape my logical train of thought, call it morality if you will, that I could not allow another human individual to go through whatever happened to those people whom my mother spied upon when they were eventually caught. I had no certain idea, nothing had been said, but it struck me with an unequivocal conviction that any punishment was not something people generally survived. With this subconscious submission bearing down on my conscience, there was only a single unavoidable conclusion as to the action I must take.

I flicked through the rest of Stanley's file, my mind and stomach turning and churning the heavy, acidic feeling I had, and then picked up another file, casually dropping Stanley's file onto the glass table a metre or so in front of the sofa. I picked up another but couldn't read the words through the forest of worries and fears, battling to stem the flood of tears that was bearing against my eyeballs.

"So what punishments do these people get?" I casually asked, off-handed with my body language.

"I don't know." She said with what I believe was an honest belief at the time.

"Do you ever see them again- like on that screen?"

A deadly silence created from that moment a permanent and uncrossable void between my mother and me, as I tried to catch her eye, she deliberately avoided me by picking something out of her bottom desk draw. Her stubborn refusal just created a chain of more questions in my thoughts to which I could only surmise answers.

"The ceremony is at 12pm, so I'll run you back home after that and we can grab some lunch." I peeked a look at my watch and my whole body seemed to slump slightly; it was barely 11am.

"Can I listen to those people on that thing?"

"Sure, yeah let me just..." My mother stumbled to find the remote under the surprising deluge of paper that had engulfed her desk since we had entered the room, my catching her unaware.

"So show me. How do you do it?"

She grabbed a couple of pads, a couple of pens and skipped around the desk to settle next to me on the sofa, which backed on to her desk.

"Sometimes, you can't quite make out what they're saying because the sound quality can be patchy. You see that coke can on the top shelf. Top right hand corner? That's the microphone."

"How did you get it there?" I was astonished at the mundane appearance of the technology.

"The shopkeeper is handsomely paid and incredibly loyal to the President. See the guy hanging around the cards at the back of the shop? That's one of my guys. He's assigned to follow that woman, all day and everyday….." The grey-haired woman, seemed ordinary; milk, bread, eggs, cheese and other groceries laid out on the counter between her and the grocer.

"Until when?"

"We catch her out."

"How many people are you watching?"

"About 10,000." Her manner was almost off hand.

"And how many agents for each one?"

"Over the lifetime of an op between 15 and 20. At a time, 3."

"How long do these last?"

"The most recent one that I concluded lasted for 20 years. She was difficult- but she slipped up in the end."

"Wow."

"You'll notice all our agents are extraordinarily ordinary. Can you remember what the last one was like?"

I tried to picture him in my mind, but in the scene captured on camera there was a bluish greyish blur. Even the woman's face had blended into anonymity.

"It has taken me a while, to learn to spot them. Here have a pen, and a list of buzzwords." She flicked a single sheet of A4 paper at me on which there was a single column of words.

"Generally, we're spotting, counting, every time the target says any of these words. If they say them all in a single sentence then I send an alarm to the Agent who picks them up, through this buzzer on the remote."

"Are all the buzzwords the same for each target?"

"No, because each individual has slightly different aims and they'll use different language."

I had lived with the certain belief that I was living my life with liberty and without hindrance and this facade had now finally been demolished. Now I was precariously balanced on the precipice with two options; to go back and accede to these lies or to drop forever without any knowledge of any real alternative. I watched and listened to the targets in a show of concentration and focus, hoping to instil a sense of confidence in my mother. I looked at the buzzwords set out on the white laminated card; blood droplets on snow, the contrast was great, but the words surprised me:

"Country

People

Class

President

Hope

Future

Way
Free
Home
Children
Join
Unite
Community
Humanity
Vote"

I had been expecting names and places, words relating to specific aims and intents, plots, conspiracies, threats of violence even. I could see a tacit link between the words but these words could be used in isolation in most innocent conversations. They were vague, general, almost normal, so unthreatening. Determined to make the most of my opportunity, I listed the words on my pad, noted the date and time and commenced work.

The time went quickly once I had got over the shock of what I was doing and the appointed time for my mother's ceremony soon arrived. She looked up from the computer, flashed a look at me and dug around in her desk. Mirror, hair brush and make up, quick touch-ups and we were off.

"You won't be able to sit with me, I'll be up the front and you'll be at the side. You won't be on your own, there will be other guests." She almost talked to herself as we hurried along.

"Great, I'm ready when you are." I steeled myself against my natural instincts to flee.

"Well, let's go then." She stepped smartly from behind the desk, rising elegantly from her chair.

My mother seemed to be itching to get there, but she relaxed her gait to enable me to stride along beside her without too much trouble. I was amazed that all morning she hadn't stammered once, "This must be something she is looking forward to" I thought. Back along the dark marble halls, star lights winking at me, we took the elevators to the very top floor; to the Grand Chamber. We had heard about the Chamber in our general studies classes, where model citizens were acknowledged, appreciated and applauded. No-one in my class apart from Louisa's parents had been to the Grand Chamber, if I recall correctly, they received awards for conduct excelling their citizenship duties. I pondered this fact, with what relevance it might have, as the elevator zoomed upwards, racing to the azure sky peeking down through the glass ceiling of the elevator shaft.

The elevator opened onto a blindingly dazzling floor of white marble with more lights in the ceiling. I had to squint. At the end of the wide hallway, in front of the heavy oak doors with marble panels and bold brass handles, sentinels in black suits and red ties supervised the doors. As we approached, they nodded quickly and sharply at my mother and pulled the doors to them to reveal a semi circle shaped room of windows, floor to ceiling, creating a glorious panoramic view of the city that could never be rivalled. The glass roof sloped from the wall which extended about three metres above the doors, to the windows so that the warm natural light bathed the whole room, the sky was almost falling into the Chamber. There were three sets of chairs; a block in the middle of the room facing out towards the city and a block either side facing into the centre of the room. The blocks on either side were square and of nine chairs each, and the block in the centre were two rows of three. A hostess, dressed with panache in a flowing and beautifully tailored silver silk trouser suit stepped forward lightly and guided my mother to her seat in the centre and then me to mine on the right hand side, the hostess's shiny, sleek black hair reflected the glare of the sun harshly. We were the first to arrive.

Over the next few minutes, the room filled rapidly with men and women, but there were no other young people or children. I felt uniquely special, permitted to witness an adult rite that as far as I knew, Louisa hadn't even seen. Infused with my smugness and restraining my self-importance, a guilt and eagerness to ensure I remembered everything I could bore down on the bottom of my stomach. My teeth were gritted with a determined concentration that my mother mistook for sympathetic nervousness and the other adults misguidedly but patronisingly thought as precocity. I was happy to let them think that, if it meant that they would leave me alone and the farce seemed to succeed.

Quite quickly all the seats were full at which point everyone fell silent and still, waiting, watching, a noiseless energy surging through the muted groups of participants. A loud burst through the polished oak doors announced the presentation party which to everyone's astonishment, and my horror, included the President.

The President was a slight man, dark but thinning hair with small rectagonal rimless glasses that seemed to enlarge the penetrating green eyes, peering out from behind the reflective lenses. His head seemed slightly too large for his body, clad in a black silk mandarin jacket with black trousers and polished lace-up shoes. The only hint of colour was the red edging to the collar of his jacket. He slithered across the floor, through the room in the midst of a small swarm of bodies; guards and aides, eyeing the various groups protectively and suspiciously. As they approached the front, all but the President split into two groups which parted in opposite directions. Perhaps the bodyguards felt that the Grand Chamber was high enough so that there was little risk of prospective assailants crashing through the window to carry out their murderous intents. The President faced the city, surveying the throbbing urban mass of buildings, machines and noise with paternal satisfaction and pride before slowly turning to the matter in hand. The special chosen ones were laid out before him in two neat rows of three. Three ladies, three gentlemen. An eon seemed to lapse before he addressed the silent, waiting Grand Chamber, non-committedly passing those venomous eyes over his attentive congregation.

"Ladies and Gentlemen," he paused. "Citizens. Welcome to Building 13, not just the heart of our nation, but our brain too. I hope that you have all enjoyed the opportunity to experience Building 13 and catch a glimpse of our day to day life here of running the Country and protecting you all.

Being a member of our nation bestows both great benefits and enormous responsibility but there is a sinister, subversive element permeating the undercurrents of our society. We are all aware of these who enjoy the benefits without bearing their share of the burden. On this great day I shall not dwell on such parasites, suffice it to say that they shall not succeed as long as we have such dedicated and loyal staff intent on bringing them in. This is then a fitting tribute to our first nominee, Amanda Smythe, a brilliant lawyer who has caught many enemies of our state as the senior legal advisor in our Intelligence Team. Amanda works tirelessly on identifying those selfish individuals who choose not to subscribe to our society and our agreed ways, those who think that they are above others, who refuse to contribute to our community but whose existence entirely depends on our benevolence and tolerance. I know that it is difficult but one of the most challenging aspects is the securing of evidence against these isolationists. For your loyalty, dedication and good conscience, Amanda, I thank you on behalf of the nation."

And so the rituals began. I didn't know if he wrote his own speeches but it seemed to me that this wasn't just a "thank you"; this was the propagation of his bilious views, the vicious and subtle indoctrination of another generation. The way in which he used my mother, as an example of this self-righteous ideology created a deep rooted, burning revulsion for this venomous little man with big statements. His introductory speeches for each nominee followed a similar vein until he had thanked each for their loyalty, dedication and good conscience, whatever that meant.

The President asked my mother to stand, to place her hand in his and to swear an oath of allegiance. Childlike, she almost jumped to her feet, presented her hands to him and inhaled deeply before reciting. "I Amanda Smythe do solemnly, sincerely and truly declare my allegiance to the President of my nation state and unequivocally and irrevocably promise to uphold, obey and promote the doctrine of good citizenship in life and death. This is my vow."

My mother spoke slowly and evenly, taking her time, pronouncing her syllables clearly and maintaining an even but constant eye contact with the President. She reached the end without mishap and the President nodded briefly, smiled at her before he moved onto the next Nominee as her beaming gaze followed him.

Eventually all of the nominees had been sworn into this self serving cult. "Thank you for your allegiance, ladies, gentlemen and citizens. That is the formal part of the ceremony completed. There are refreshments along the wall at the back, please help yourself." He turned to face the city again, the early afternoon sunlight caught some of the windows of the nether buildings and sparkled up at us, and as we stood to rise and walk away our attention was held as he turned and added "But please remember that throughout the rest of their lives your loved ones will need your help, support and love in upholding their vows of citizenship. I trust that you will not let them down." He crossed his hands, one over the other in front of him and bowed cleanly and crisply at us; the ceremony was over. He had given us barely thirty minutes of his precious time before he hand-shaked his way through his disciples to depart the room.

As a reward I suppose, my mother allowed me the rest of the day away from school. She didn't come into the house with me, just stopped the car at the drive long enough for me to get out. "Have fun! I'll see you later." Her departing words hung in the thickening summer air.

Chapter 9

I felt disgusted, soiled and abused at the way in which I had been incorporated into the ceremony on the brazen assumption that my love and pride for my mother overruled everything else I might think, see or feel. I raced up to my room, stripped and surged into the shower to scrub the makeup and hair mousse from me as well. This was just not me. Time passed while I stood there, letting the gentle jet of water break over me, feeling my thoughts float around me in the shower cubicle as I made my decision. Another one of those compass points in life, except this time I knew that this was a vital moment in my past, present and future as I dressed into jeans, t-shirt, jumper and trainers, packed my day sack with spare clothes, pen-knife, torch and wallet and left my mobile and diary on the bed. I slowly removed the pearl earrings that had been my confirmation present, the silver necklace that I had been given when I got an "A" in my general studies and the bracelet from my shaking wrist, the one that my mother had given to me when she returned to work. I dropped them deliberately into the bin, in a private ceremony.

I felt alive with the conscious choice that I was making. My skin prickled when I wrapped my scarf around my neck, pulled my waterproof fleece on to my shoulders and shoved my hat and gloves into my pockets, the blood that pulsated through my veins caused my fingers to tremble. I didn't feel any great need to write a note, I supposed my mother would work it out quickly enough.

I have not seen my mother since that hazy summer afternoon. It seems that I betrayed her and the President, but it now appears that my rebellion against the latter was something for which she could and would never forgive me. She felt it so keenly that she didn't attend Court when I was tried nor when I was convicted, she refused to see me when I was captured and sent to the psychiatric hospital and would not see me upon my release. My social worker had tried to contact her without my knowledge, she thought it would help but I knew I had made my decision and would have to live with the consequences. Hence, as I write this only the social worker has seen me since my release. I have since come to terms with her absence, but the loss of Alex and Ben still echoes throughout my consciousness; it resonates like a tolling bell during the harshest winter's morning.

As I left the house for what turned out to be the last time, I pulled the door shut and pushed my keys back through the letter box, thanking my lucky stars that most views of the door were blocked by the neatly trimmed privet hedge.

The weakening sun was beginning to sink slowly in the lingering warmth of the late afternoon as I sat on an old battered red bus that was heading into town before nervously disembarking at the market square. When I headed north and walked for half an hour along prim city residential streets, I briefly worried about what I was doing but just as quickly I firmly reassured myself that this was the only way I could reconcile who I was with what I wanted. The vision of Stanley in the red file had confirmed that I could not subscribe to this society as it was.

The wrought iron gates of St. Augustine's loomed at the end of the pretty suburban street that I had been striding along. They were dark and heavy, erected to keep the local comprehensive trash out and lend some gravitas to the grounds. I walked past the gates to find a place I could safely and guardedly watch the gates as it was now approaching kicking out time for the boys. I wondered if I should have left a diversionary message for my mother, perhaps implying that I had gone to Louisa's but I realised how obtuse that particular idea was and reflected with relief that I hadn't done so and that any note of my disappearance would depend entirely on when my mother returned home from work.

An eerie, groaning, wrenching sound in the silent peace caught my attention and the gates were pulled back by an old, white haired man in a black overcoat, grey flat cap, almost shepherd like both in appearance and manner. It seemed to take a moment or too for the flock to come but the boys soon surged through the gates and I felt my blood race.

I spotted Philip as he meandered across the road, ambling in my vague direction. It hadn't taken long for the throngs to dissipate into the locality and I moved away slowly following Philip, touching his elbow to catch his attention.
"Yes, huh, oh hi!" He stammered in surprise. "What are you….. What's the matter?" he caught the urgency and tension in my face.
"Keep walking, let's find somewhere open, but private." I muttered. He looked mildly confused and perplexed at my intensity but nodded for me to follow him. We crossed busy roads and wandered down dirty alleyways, behind grand houses, before we came to a large open field. It might have

been a playground once, but the equipment had been removed a long time ago. The grass was still neat and short, someone was clearly keeping it tidy as surprisingly there was no litter at all and as we approached the centre I felt easier because I could see everything in a circle for a clear 150 metres.

Philip hugged me and whispered "I heard about your dad. I just didn't know what to do. I'm really sorry that I wasn't there for you."
"Please don't worry about it." I looked to him intently with sincerity. "There is something else we need to worry about." Bewilderment streaked across his face, he allowed me to explain all that I had seen and heard. Slowly his confusion became comprehension and then it turned to concern.
"Oh god. How do we deal with this? My mother and father will never understand, this is unforgivable."
"You are not going to tell them are you?" I said sharply, instantaneously regretting my tone. It was immediately apparent that Philip didn't share my sense of indignation at what our society had become.
"Of course I am, I can do nothing else. My parents are loyal citizens, they humoured Stanley with his writing and stories, when I said that it would come to bring misfortune." I searched his eyes for a clue or sign, to reassure me that I was misunderstanding but there was nothing.

"Do you know where exactly he is?" He demanded.

"No, I couldn't tell from the file." I answered calmly. A complete lie born solely out of Phillip's attitude.

"Well, I have to go. I'm meeting Louisa soon." He said shortly, not realising what he had let slip. I stared at him trying not to react, not to do anything stupid.

"Ah, I am sorry that came out like that. I did mean to tell you, rather, Louisa was supposed to tell you. It's just that you didn't get in touch until now. I thought that it was over and anyway, my parents weren't keen."

"Oh?"

"Well, after your father's death. They knew he was an accountant, they heard about the money difficulties, so to speak and well….. There were the rumours…. Um…" he started to clam up. I tried to relax, I needed to hear whatever Philip was going to say.

"It's okay, I understand, tell me." I gently prodded him.

"You really need to be careful. There are rumours about your father's death; that it wasn't an accident. And…well….the rumours implicate you, that you led your father to his death."

I desperately tried to remain calm, to not cry, to keep control. I shrugged my shoulders care freely.

"Well, they're just rumours." I surmised.

"But they can get you into a lot of trouble. I've got to go, be careful." He warned with a fraternal hand on my shoulder. Then he turned and headed back alone, the way we had come.

I sat down heavily on the soft, gentle grass. So people now thought that I had deliberately goaded my father into chasing me and running into the road? A recollection surfaced in my head about a story we had heard in Current Affairs. A mother had told her daughter that she wished that the daughter had never been born, and had consequently been convicted of causing death by reckless speech when the daughter had thrown herself in front of a train. My distant memory told me that the woman had been subsumed into the prison system after her conviction. Although I hadn't truly and honestly confronted my own involvement in my father's death, the certainty that I could not return home struck me with ferocious force along with the idea that if I found Stanley then my situation would be stronger

I lay flat on my back in that field for a few hours until dusk began to fall and the afternoon warmth began to disperse into the purple shades of the darkening sky. I needed to know where Stanley was, the area, the town, something. A wild idea formed in my head and I went to find a telephone.

"Hi Mum, it's me. I've gone shopping, in town. What time will you be home?"

"Late." I could tell she was she was distracted by something.

"Okay…..oh my god! Mum! That bloke! Coming out of that

shop. He looks just like one of those guys in the files today."

"Which one?" Her tone was sharp, her attention now complete.

"The skin-headed one. Was his name Steve or something?"

"You mean Stanley Sanderson?"

"Yeah."

"Impossible, he's up north in Whitley Bay. But I'll get my guys to check it out. Good work darling."

"Well, sorry I didn't mean to disturb you."

"No, that's okay. I'd rather be safe and check than…, look I've got to go. See you later."

"Yeah, okay." And the line went dead.

It had been a huge risk but it had worked and now I had a target, but finding Stanley would be difficult and I had to really hope that the authorities didn't get to him first or me for that matter, but at this point I was unaware of the trouble that I was in.

I had enough cash in my wallet to buy me a ticket for the overnight bus to Berwick upon Tweed, almost 350 miles away. I didn't really know what my mother would do when she realised that I had gone, I knew it wouldn't be for at least a couple hours before she got home. Who knew after that? I had to leave town quickly and anonymously.

The bus station was busy when I got there, people queuing bustling and waiting. Lots of young people were milling around, some travelling, some off to visit relatives and others just for the sake of being somewhere. I was given my ticket by a bored inattentive man, probably a student, as he didn't ask me any questions when I volunteered no information, a practice I would observe relentlessly. There wasn't a great amount of time before the bus left after I'd bought my ticket and so I headed straight to the relevant bus stand. There was no-one else other than the driver waiting, so I hung around behind people at the adjacent stand, until he started the bus. I made a dash for it.

"Hurry up Miss! Where's your ticket?" He demanded grumpily. I handed it over meekly.

"You're a bit young?"

"Off to see my dad. Parents have separated see." I sat down and waved, madly and energetically, a big grin on my face. A kind middle aged woman with a toddle waved back at me. They probably thought I was some pathetic teenager, sentimental at the thought of leaving town. If the truth is to be told, I was desperately scared but it seemed to placate the driver though, who nodded at the stranger and at me, and then we left each other to it.

I dozed fitfully on and off throughout the journey, briefly opening my eyes when I sensed we had stopped and people were getting on or off. When I couldn't doze, I stared out of the window and allowed my thoughts to take on a life of their own. I imagined the best outcome and the worst scenario when I found Stanley, my mother located me or worse the rumours caught up with me. I couldn't bear the idea of the rumours being right; it didn't make sense to me.

Louisa's parents had known that my father and I had argued, although the source of their information was far from clear as was the extent of such knowledge. Everyone at school knew that Louisa's parents were some of the Favoured Few; well connected with the President and his administration and my concern was as what they might decide to do with their suspicions, however tenuous. As with so many issues in my life, the statutes were far from clear; murder by reason of incitement to death- what did that mean? I could not deny that my father and I had argued loudly and aggressively- certainly on my part- and that, in a culmination of the sense of failure and intense fear, I had said what I had said to him. Until that morning I had had a life many children would never have the opportunity to appreciate, that had been provided by my parents and it was the inherent fear that accompanies foreboding change that brought my world crashing down around me so catastrophically. A huge sense of guilt engulfed me (a burden now eased by time, experience and my recollections) but at that time my certainty surrounding my father's accident as to whether I really saw him deliberately step into the road, began to waver. I had watched old television programmes in which similar arguments had been depicted and in the broadcasts "I wish you were dead" seemed to be a typical teenage retort. The single deviation between the fiction and my factual situation was that my father had actually died very shortly after. I could understand the interest in which the Presidential Guard might want to take in my case, but I could do nothing if my father had chosen to end his life. It seemed entirely unfair that I could be punished for something I had no power to prevent.

It wasn't what I thought society was about; feelings and emotions being held to account, thoughts and ideas being dangerous, but then when did I ever have free thought? And then it struck me, school was not the exchange of thoughts and ideas that it should have been, we were always directed along a path, herded over obstacles and chaperoned through the gates.

Now, it seems strange how significant such events in my life have become, even funnier how I didn't realise that they were just that at the time they occurred. I remember becoming attuned to subtle changes in my life that is to say that I was able to recognise something meaningful. I was still not yet worldly enough to appreciate what these shifts in balance, movements in relationships and switches of emphasis might mean and how they might interchange. My own knowledge and awareness was beginning to develop into something more global, a fact nodded at by the educational authorities as we started to engage in debates at school about current affairs. The definition of "current affairs" was itself defined not by events worthy of intellectual debate, but by our teachers, something no-one else in my class noticed.

"Class, in today's lesson we're going to have a discussion about the media. Today's question is whether, there is a place for independent media groups in today's society." A buzz of bored chatter rippled around the hive of the bleak cold classroom.
"You have 10 minutes to formulate your arguments. This side of the class will argue that there is a need for independent media groups and rest of you will present the case against such a need."
For the stipulated time, my mind wandered through a myriad of ideas in which the central theme was not clear, no matter how linked this vague network of connections seemed to me. The longer those thoughts dwelled, the more suspicious I became of the question; what was it they wanted me to say? I pondered the basic idea of free speech, how an exchange of ideas worked and the concept of an individual's role in society. A peculiar image formed vaguely at the back of my mind;

those green eyes on that pitted face below the shaved head stared at me from within my own mind.

"Caroline?"

"We have no need for independent media groups. In the past such groups caused confusion and unnecessary consternation in society. They argued for freedom of speech when such freedom caused divisive debate between sections of the population on issues such as fox-hunting, smoking, childcare and justice. Such organisations used the idea of freedom of speech to publish sensationalist, controversial and populist articles whose only purpose was to increase circulation and further the groups' private capitalist ideologies. In today's society, where we have two media organisations who represent the political parties we have an open discourse on a diverse range of topics." Caroline completed her oratory with a crisp finish, a hint of smugness breathed across her face as she settled back into her chair and shook her head, swinging her long fair hair superiorly across her shoulders, the individual strands moved as one, the lighting catching glistening grains along them.

"Thank you Caroline, Lizzie?"

"I would endorse all that Caroline said but also I would like to pick up on her point about sensationalism. These media organisations fuelled a whole industry of nasty, manipulative individuals who used money, drugs, sex, greed and vanity to trap unwilling and unsuspecting public figures. Such figures would be held up as idols of moral ineptitude, examples of what not to do, humiliated and stripped of their dignity. There were many examples of these people suffering emotional turmoil with the breakdown of marriages, the creation of rifts between siblings and the distasteful instigation of public feuds. These disputes would invariably lead to arguments in the Court. The huge amount of money wasted in lawyers fees, is a side product but the real issues are the hurt, anguish and distress caused to everyone involved." The poisonous sense of righteous indignation began to curdle the breakfast milk in my stomach.

"A good point well made. Georgia?"

"We are expected to be loyal to the President, in return for our loyalty and faith, he will look after us. There is no need for independent media organisations." The final nail in the coffin, concisely made in a sharp tone that was forced through the long pointed nose on the frighteningly pale face framed by the sleek bobbed hair.

Our teacher smiled smugly, surveying her protégés proudly. An unknown quantity, Ms Clarke lived at the school and as far as anyone knew, she had no husband or boyfriend. There had been no mention of family or indeed of a background made within shot of our ultra perceptive ears. We would watch her stride, her steps in regular marching time, across the school courtyard to the Residence at the end of the long morning, signalled by the relieving shrill of the lunch bell. No pupil had ever been known in all of the school's history to have crossed the threshold of the Residence. It was fortified with its only look-out in the form of Mr Roberts; the teacher's porter. His eyesight, hearing and sense of foreboding trouble were keener than any student. Having nodded curtly to Mr Roberts, Ms Clarke would then disappear into the dark depths of the unknown for a few moments before emerging at the French doors on the first floor. Still as an eagle surveying its quarry and equally as sharp-eyed, her profile menacingly stark against the sky, she would watch, almost jealously, her pupils milling around the courtyard, chatting and laughing. With her hands clasped around her middle, standing militarily straight and erect, almost rigid in whatever weather was thrown at her, it didn't appear to bother her that beneath her intense watch most of the giggling arose from cruel jokes about her, her face remained passively blank.

"Fenn?" Ms Clarke's deep, plummy tones addressed me directly. My nerves pounded my ribcage as I began to set out my indefensible position; recklessly unsure and unconcerned about the consequences.

"We are all human beings. We have the same physical features; two eyes, ears, nose, heart, lungs and brain. But we are all very different in our own ways because we have an ability to think rationally. Our souls make our existence more than just that and our brains allow us to appreciate this. We are all capable of independent thought and nothing can stop us doing so. The lack of independent media organisations does not matter as long as each of us is able to think for ourselves. I suppose in that sense it is irrelevant whether or not independent media organisations exist."

The teacher's left eyebrow raised in a direct, angular fashion straining against the tautness of her face, pulled by the tight bun of hair, fixed at the back of Ms Clarke's head.

"Surely thought depends on what you know?" Her voice began to pitch threateningly, tailing off into a velvet hush.

"Yes, it is, which is why our education is crucial, but we must not close our minds to other influences. An independent media organisation would challenge existing principles and ideas, to create truly open discussion and debate which would encourage us all to think." The room had gone remarkably silent, my fellow classmates were staring at me; I was some rabid mongrel that had slipped in amongst the pedigree poodles.

"But the President thinks for us. Our membership in society is in return for sacrifice of our individual rights. Your trust and faith in the President will be rewarded." I received the short lecture from the teacher with a curt re-assuring nod of my head. "Well done, you did well to argue an impossible case so eloquently." She added, her tone lightening considerably, having decided there was no harm that had been done and that the debate could be ended safely.

"Hands up, if you're voting "Yes", we do need independent

media organisations?"

One hand.

Mine.

And if you're voting "no"?" Everyone else's hands went up.

The classroom resembled an eerie picture of dead trees rising out of a flooded plain. I surveyed the carnage of democracy and noted my teacher scribbling a note, hastily folding it into her bag, glancing surreptitiously in my direction. The clock ticked on and in the distance the bell signalled the end of the lesson; I fled the tension, quietly, calmly and without outward sign of the inner storm that had engulfed me.

"Hey Fenn!" Georgia's voice carried down the corridor gaily. "Wait up!"

"I'm off to the bog, I'll see you in Maths." I shouted back brusquely before scurrying off to the toilets at the end of the packed hot and noisy hallway, through the swaying throng of girls. The door banged loudly against the cool whitewashed walls when I barged through the doorway, startling the first year girls who quickly fled, leaving the bathroom behind them silently empty. It was a refreshing relief to the intense anarchy outside. A sharp pain had begun to attack me from within the deep crevices of my brain, pounding the back of my eyeballs with all its might. At the same time an oppressive tightness had enveloped my neck and shoulders so that I felt I was being pressed inwards from my sides, a sense of claustrophobia muffled anything else I could possibly feel. I bumped my way into a cubicle and dropped heavily onto the toilet seat which buckled slightly under the impact. An early summer breeze breathed through the open window, gusting the claustrophobia away so that the pressure from my sides eased and I could see my thoughts again. Was I missing something? Or did everyone else really believe that the President should think for us? What did they know that I didn't? I couldn't work it out- to me it seemed an affront that someone should tell me what to think, do or say. What did it matter if I disagreed with someone? It, at the very least, created a conversation and at the most made life interesting. I re-played Ms Clarke's voice in my head; the admonishing way in which she had put the proposition to me, the threat to which I had meekly submitted, perhaps subconsciously aware that to rebel would bring consequences that I was simply not prepared for. The chattering sounds and multitude of footsteps ended as quickly as it started, doors slammed at the start of the next lesson making me realise that I had to hurry to maths.

Chapter 10

As the bus rumbled onwards, I noticed the brickwork of the houses darken and the style of the houses become austere, although I didn't know precisely where the bus was. The roads were empty as the bus meandered up the country. Away from the hustle of the motorways the villages became further and further apart and were engulfed for the most part in darkness and silence, just the headlights to guide us and the intermittent, crackling interruption of the driver's radio. I wasn't panicking yet because I hadn't heard anything relating to me, although it struck me that they might be waiting for me in Liverpool but then I thought I was just being paranoid, still in the end I got off the bus at Ashington, way, before the bus's final stop leaving the driver in bored solitude to push on through the lifting mist.

It was now 5am and the dawn colours were trickling into the cloudy sky, streaks of amber, purple and yellow filtering upwards from the horizon. An icy, bitter breeze sliced across the bleak bus station, which was a grey concrete warehouse perched precariously on the edge of the town. I was the sole passenger to get off onto the deserted concourse, no-one else in sight but a couple of beer cans dancing in the wind, twisting and turning noisily across the concrete floor. The cold warehouse was beginning to flood with sunlight, not enough to warm the air, as I heard a low, murmured chatter coming from a drivers' café, on the corner at the entrance to the bus station. A place where people to go until a more decent hour.

I slipped through the door into a square hut that had been temporary once upon a time, filled with a dozen oblong school desks and accompanying wooden frame chairs. The walls bore cream windows dressed with green gingham curtains and the floor was covered with polished green linoleum. All clean and neat, but the smell of grease clung to everything and permeated the warmth emanating from the box radiators. A counter ran the length of one wall, with two middle aged women standing guard. One was short, slight with short spiky hair, the other was taller, with a round face and soft curly hair, her rosy cheeks speckled with freckles. About half of the tables were filled, most with large burly men in uniforms, bearing the names of different bus companies. I was completely ignored until I reached the counter, and the taller lady served me my cup of hot chocolate and my blueberry muffin with a silent nod and a curt smile.

There was an empty table in the corner near the window that I chose; it looked out of the bus station so I was able to see any traffic in either direction. Occasional delivery trucks trundled along the tired tarmac, followed by short convoys of cars, slowed by up by heavy cumbersome loads. Someone had left their newspaper on the table and I flicked casually through the battered rag whilst I picked at the muffin and let the steaming chocolate cool slightly. The newspaper was a local one with photographs of children's fancy dress competitions, dog shows and various pillars of the community. There were also a lot of adverts for local businesses, for jobs and sales, open days and discounts. When I got to the end I went back to the start and read each article and advert carefully, noting how every so often sentences didn't quite make sense, as if something had been taken out or added in. I remembered what Philip and I had discussed, just after we had noticed Stanley's name. It became obvious that the entire publication had been meticulously reviewed and amended and it seemed ridiculous to me that a report on a village fete couldn't be published without censorship.

I mused over the issue of censorship and what the Authorities were stopping us from reading, considering, discussing, while the last dregs of my drink went cold. It seemed perverse that a democratically elected body could become so afraid of its own electorate that it imposed restrictions and requirements to safeguard its own power. A crash from the kitchen broke my dreamy stupor and I realised that I was alone, a good time to leave notwithstanding the fact that I had nowhere to go.

My intended final destination was still 20 miles away but, I guessed, that it would be safer for both Stanley and I if stayed low here for a few days before moving on. I was determined that it would not be me who would help the Presidential Guard capture Stanley and I therefore wanted to avoid anything that meant giving out my identity details. So as unobtrusively as I came, I slipped out of the café, walking purposefully from the bus station once in the open air. It occurred to me that if someone was watching me they would assume I had somewhere to go and so I slackened my pace, lengthened my gait and relaxed to appear casual. It was still too early for me to be a genuine tourist and lights were only just starting to appear in kitchens and bedrooms, the street lights went out street by street as dawn took on a more tangible effect and I needed to find somewhere to wait until I could move on. I didn't have to walk far to reach the edge of town, the bus station had been isolated anyway.

The land surrounding this town was flat, prim hedges, neatly divided fields and crops, and a long road travelled north to south. If I headed south I would be going back on myself, and whilst that might bring additional protection, I could see outlying buildings to the north, whether they were inhabited or not I could not tell but the walk would kill time. I set off north, trying to maintain my leisurely relaxed stroll, whilst constructing an excuse or reason for why I might be wandering along such a solitary road at such a time. The road was eerily silent from the moment I set off, as I saw no cars, lorries, tractors or any other person on the road. The bitter breeze ran from east to west although the rising sun warmed me a little, but other than me, the brutally awakening wind was my only other companion on the road, so much so I was slightly unnerved as I approached my target.

As it turned out, the buildings formed a farm. Devoid of any life whether human or animal, it bore signs that this until recently had been a working environment. I stepped quietly and carefully through the yard, noting the tractor abandoned midway through a change of tyre, the grain store that had been left open so that the breezes had liberally scattered the grain across the cobbled surface of the yard and the putrid stench emanating from the dairy which suggested the last milking of the cows had been left unfinished. It was clear to me that something had happened, but what I could not tell. At the back of the yard was a beautiful old, wise-looking, stone farmhouse, watching over the rest of the farm. It had three storeys with the old sash style windows that looked as if they had been recently repainted in a brilliant white gloss.

As I got closer through the wildly dispersed buckets and disarray of the yard and outbuildings, the farmhouse no longer looked noble and benevolent as it certainly once had, it now seemed ramshackle, embarrassed and ashamed at its condition. The huge oak arched door had been felled so that it was lying on its back in the middle of the large, dark, echoing hallway and many of the windows on the ground floor had been smashed, indiscriminately. Pinned to the doorframe was a blank cream envelope and after checking no one was around I unpinned it and untucked the flap. The letter with was brief, the scripted date in the right hand corner indicating that it had been hurriedly scribbled a fortnight previously:-

"Dear Tom and Mary,

We are so sorry to hear about your troubles. We have taken the cattle and sheep to our farm for safekeeping until your return.

If there is anything we can do, just let us know.

Yours truly

Peter and Jane"

I folded the letter and returned it to the envelope, repining it in the same small hole. Instantly, the carnage became apparent when I ventured across the threshold of the house. The beautifully graceful antique grandfather clock had had its glass face smashed, a deep scratch lacerated the walnut casing, papers and photos were cruelly scattered throughout the deep passageway. A dark mahogany table lay on its side with a leg splintered in two and its drawer spilling its secrets onto the carpet. Intruding into a scene of a battle that caused such horror, I paused briefly and then stepped further into the hallway. I peered through the hallway and could see a kitchen, towards which I stepped gently and hesitantly. Off both sides of the hallway there were a number of rooms; an office, a sitting room, a library and a dining room, each of whom had been brutally assaulted and left to fester in chaos. The kitchen however was even worse, primarily because of the trail of blood across the stone floor and whitewashed walls. The stretched stains of blood on the walls demonstrated that someone had resisted hard, dragging their fingers across the wall and I could see a clearly defined handprint on the frame of the backdoor that had been left hanging from its hinges forsaking the kitchen to the trespassing elements from the garden.

No matter what mind tricks they played on me in the hospital, nothing will ever relieve me of the horror of the garden. Such traumatic visions have remained with me and will, I fear, continue to do so forever; certainly as long as the ghosts of those martyrs remain betrayed and vengeful. I do not expect you to understand, the times have changed, for my part, I know it is for the worse. But it will change.

I intrepiditiously crept through the kitchen, retching with revulsion at events which I could only suspect had happened. The farmer and his wife were initially attacked in the hallway by assailants who had seemingly forced entry into the house; the couple had then tried to flee through the kitchen but were either chased or cut off. I looked at the walls of the kitchen and found tiny pock-marks in the walls, the tell-tale shells that had laid fallow by the kitchen door confirmed the firing of rifles. The couple had still been struggling as they were dragged from the kitchen into the once beautifully cultivated garden, where onions, leeks, lettuces, carrots and beans had been nurtured. Only they and their assailants knew what happened between leaving the kitchen and the final moments of their lives but I stood in the doorway of the kitchen momentarily staring at the smouldering piles of what looked like books and papers, but on top of which were the unmistakable remains of two naked bodies, charred and contorted beyond recognition. Even from my basic level of anatomy I could tell that one of the victims had been shot through the knee caps, whilst the fingers on the other looked stubby and misshapen. I dared not imagine what had happened. But I did know this; that the smell of burning human flesh is as bad as they say it is.

Blind with panic, fear and disgust I ran to a flower bed and vomited profusely. How long I stayed there on my knees, wobbling and shaking, my stomach muscles tightly contracted, I do not know but I heard the aptly mournful song of a bird and began to gather myself together. I could not look at the pile any longer as I returned to the house. I hurried though the kitchen; back into the hallway and up the stairs. There was an immediate contrast; the assailants, whoever they might have been, had not come up stairs. It seemed that they had found everything they had wanted downstairs.

On the first floor at the top of the stately oak staircase, there was a master bedroom with an en-suite bathroom. The bed was neatly made, the curtains drawn back and held back by their matching ties, and a faint, lingering smell of fresh laundry hung about the room. There were photographs on the bedside table of a family of five, perhaps ready for framing, the date on the back was a month ago. A tall and lean man of about fifty with sandy hair and a strong jaw stood at the back of the group, a lady about the same age, short and wiry with short black hair alongside him, and then there were three girls crowded into the front of the frame; all blonde, all tall and lean, ranging from 20 to 30 years of age.

Three other bedrooms were also on the first floor, all which still bore with proud sentiment the wooden name plates attached to their doors, on which one said Elizabeth and had a dog on it, one said Sarah and had a cat on it and the other said Kathryn and that one had a horse on it. Time had eaten away at the edges of the name plates, leaving them slightly worn and cracked. Each of these rooms were painted in a different colour but were unmistakably rooms that had retained their childlike qualities despite their occupants having moved on. What had happened to these girls? Had they been involved in the savage raid upon their family home? I couldn't tell but the pristine nature of the first floor induced an angry sadness in me at the reality that such a beautiful loving family existence could be destroyed so completely by such violence and brutality. With this anger burning and raging I carried on with my tour, climbing the narrow stairs to the second floor, which consisted of two homely guest rooms, so obviously having been made up for warmly welcomed visitors no matter if they might call unannounced. Both rooms had views from the front and back of the house from which I could see for miles around. I wandered among my thoughts as I scanned the vacant, bland horizon, musing whether if the farmer and his wife had stayed up here, would they have seen their attackers coming and been able to escape? It was irrelevant now and would do no more than to fuel my rage.

I spent the next few days in the house, sleeping in one of the guest bedrooms, eating pasta and rice from the kitchen and exploring what was left of the office and library. I learned that the daughters had all emigrated, or perhaps escaped, to Canada with their own families and from their letters it appeared that they had eventually tried to persuade their parents to do the same before Canada had shut its border to us.

From the littered papers strewn everywhere it became clear that the farmer had been in politics before he had retired. I saw cuttings from newspapers with pictures of him with previous prime ministers, but I could find no reason for his apparent early retirement. Fragments of letters from other retired politicians in which they expressed their concern about current policies, the attitude of younger politicians and the future of the country fluttered along the polished wood floors frivolously. Views were aired in these letters that dealt with the merging of the political parties, the gradual erosion of the right to vote on the grounds of national security and the slow grinding process of the abolition of the two houses of parliament. Many of the heavy cream envelopes were marked "By hand", evidently the writers mistrusted the national postal services. Computer cables dangled wildly from the mahogany desk, torn from the back of whatever rogue computer had been snatched away. Despite my careful search I could find no computer and guessed that it had also formed part of the bonfire or had just been confiscated.

My most shocking discovery was yet to come. Beneath the devastation, I spotted the answer phone machine buried under the mess in the hallway. I carefully and respectfully picked through the carnage and although the casing was cracked, perhaps stamped upon, it still worked. It was an older model that still relied on a cassette tape. I set it up in my room and, my hand trembling, pressed play with increasing terror. There were a number of messages including from the daughters checking if their parents were okay opened proceedings. Then there was a loud banging and then-
"Hello! Open up!" It is the Governmental Guard! Open Up! I'll count to five and if you don't let us in we'll break the door

down! This is an order!!"

Silence…

"1……2……3……4……5……"

There came a further silence followed by the slow rhythmic banging, a deafening lurch and then a heavy thud as, what I imagined was, the oak door thundered to the floor. Footsteps and scuffling, doors slammed, furniture being scraped across the floor, all driving a vicious shiver up my spine. A loud piercing scream of absolute fear sliced through the thickly clouded background noise, amongst more shouting.

"There! I've found her, she's in the library!" A gruff male voice called out.

Another panic-stricken scream appalled me.

"Let go of me! Who do you think you are? This is a democracy, we live in a free world. We are entitled to say what we think!! Let me go!!" The high pitch of a woman's voice cut through the rest of the cacophony of sound.

There was a sharp stinging slap.

"Let her go!" A fierce angry voice joined the melee.

A crack sounded, followed quickly by another scream.

"You are being arrested by the Presidential Governmental Guard. You are accused of being an enemy of the state, an offence punishable by death!"

"NO! On what grounds do you say that I an enemy of the state?" The man was angry but strangely rational, his voice was firm and even.

"We are not authorised to release that information." The smugness was tangible.

"That's absurd!" protested the male voice.

"Really?" A cold, cruel voice sneered. "You do not make any laws, your only obligation is to obey these laws and to be good citizens!!" He barked. "At least one of your daughters understands!"

Silence allowed this last comment to hang in the air.

"Papa, mama, don't struggle. They will kill you otherwise!" A soft voice in the distance pleaded.

"Lizzie? How could you!!" screamed the lady's voice. The force of the betrayal abundantly apparent in her tone and I could only picture her face, with enormous sadness, at having discovered her daughter's treacherous affiliations.

The awkward silence was smashed by a scuffle, a crash and more screaming. There was a smash of glass and a low chime resounded below the surface of the chaos, amid dragging and bumping, it seemed that the grandfather clock had become a victim whilst the farmer and his wife were dragged into the kitchen.

"Unless you renounce your public statements and announce your loyalty to the President you will be shot." The cruel voice calmly reassured the couple. It seemed to be closer now, this man had started to move through the house. I could see his movements, but couldn't imagine his face.

"Do it Papa, please!" Lizzie begged.

And then, softly, the farmer said "I'm sorry Lizzie, there is more at stake here than my life. I will not swear allegiance to a man who is now using fear and violence to maintain power. I do renounce all association with the man that calls himself the President." His voice never wavered and was firm through out. His wife then spoke, serenely-

"Lizzie, one day you will understand why we are taking this position. You think that you do not have a choice? Then remember the past and imagine the future."

There was more scuffling and a click. The tape had run out. What happened after that was only supposition and speculation although the bodies in the bonfire left little doubt as to how the drama had ended.

I remained hunched over the cassette player all afternoon so that my back began to ache, staring at the tape, almost willing the figures involved to come alive and explain themselves; nothing happened, except an epiphany that this tape was historical, could change the situation and perhaps make people like Lizzie realise that this democracy was no small thing and that finally I had to do something and that this would start with finding Stanley.

In the library, I found maps that the Governmental Guard had not seen fit to destroy, which set out the local area, roads and footpaths showing that it was about 15 miles to the town in which I knew that Stanley was hiding. Walkable, so I decided that I would leave just before sunset and hoped to arrive at about 9am, allowing for rest during the hike. I would walk only the footpaths, avoiding roads, populated areas and hopefully awkward questions.

Chapter 11

I walked onto the High Street at 9.30am the next morning with my feet hurting as I looked for a newsagent or the kind of shop that would display public notices and local advertisements in the window. I needed to walk for a further painful ten minutes before I found such a shop with the usual "for rent" and "for sale" notices and positions wanted. Now that I was in the vicinity of Stanley's location I needed a base from which to explore and gauge the situation which that meant getting a job with boarding, but nothing appropriate had been advertised on the aging cork pin board in the dusty window. The shop next door was a coffee shop so I popped into the newsagents quickly to buy a local newspaper and then darted back into the coffee shop for hot chocolate and a muffin. I scoured the classified pages closely and spotted only one advert with any promise, a Pick Your Own Farm, whatever that was. They seemed to offer an hourly wage with dormitory accommodation, and crucially no interview or reference was required. I need only to attend the farm shop and enquire within; the only problem was that is was two miles out of town. With heavy feet but steely resolve, I left the quickly cooled dregs of my hot chocolate and headed off.

The Farm was located on the other side of the town from which I had arrived, set back off the road and at the end of a long gravel track, which was badly kept so that weeds and grass sprouted between the small stones. Various crops of vegetables and fruit were being nurtured to maturity in the expanse of green fields which spread from the farm buildings, but I couldn't tell exactly what each of those fields would eventually yield. Three warehouse like buildings were arranged in a horse-shoe formation around a hard concrete yard, with the open side of the yard facing away from the road, open to the brutal meteorological elements that would often rampage across the flat, wild plains surrounding the farm. The track seemed to effortlessly slip between the buildings and as it did so there was situated on the end of the building on my left the farm shop with its glass veranda. The "open" sign was clearly and visibly hung on the door which was swinging slightly to and fro in the mildly warm breeze; the bell rang shrill as I pushed the door open further to step inside. The air in the glass veranda was already warm from the bright morning sun but it cooled considerably when I moved through another doorway on my left into the main body of the building in which a bare electric light bulb hung overhead, its light failing to reach the corners of the room. My eyes took a little while to adjust to the stark contrast from the brightness of the outdoors to the murky dimness inside.

"Hello there!" A lady appeared from the back of the shop, her appearance took me aback slightly with scalp that had been shaved to leave a soft velvet covering and her golden tan. "I'm Nicky, What can I do for you?" She enquired pleasantly.
"I saw your advert in the paper and wondered if you still need people?"
"Sure we do. You're a bit young though?"
"I'm 16. Does it matter, if it's legal?"
"No, I suppose not, it's just casual labour. What's your name?"
"Louisa."
"Ok, nice to meet you Louisa. When can you start?"
"As soon as you need me. Your advert mentioned accommodation?"
"Yep, no problem. You don't mind that it's mixed?"
I shook my head slightly at the thought of my school friends' ultimate fantasy, but wasn't really sure that I didn't.
"Well a couple of guys are already out there, so let me show you around, introduce you to Will and get you settled in."
I nodded enthusiastically and followed Nicky around the shop, the dormitory, the wash room and the packing shed. She told

me that they grew potatoes, carrots, lettuces, onions, tomatoes, apples, strawberries and plums. As we meandered around the farm, Nicky described what went on.

"This season we'll be picking strawberries, lettuces, tomatoes, apples. We're really lucky with the soil and water, we get some fantastically tasty crops You'll be collecting them in buckets, which will be loaded into the back of a trailer parked in the avenue between the lines. When that trailer is full, an empty one will be brought and so you can carry on picking. You'll finish at 4pm and go back to the wash room, empty the trailers, wash the fruit and then take them to be packed."

It all seemed to make perfectly good sense to me.

"Lunch will be served between 12:30pm and 2:00pm in the packing shed and cold drinks will be brought out at 10:30am and 3:00pm"

We would be expected to be in the fields at 8am Sunday to Friday and usually, depending on how much we had picked would finish at 8pm.

"Dinner will then be set out in the packing shed once you're done. I do most of the cooking and most people seem to enjoy it." Nicky chuckled to herself.

At the moment there would be twelve of us but later in the season there would be as many as thirty pickers. We ended our tour at the dormitory, which was the longest shed of the three, beds were stacked three high, each stack separated only by a wall to which were attached a hanging rail and three wardrobes. In the corner of each cubicle were a sink and a mirror.

"The toilets and showers are at the other end of the shed. I'll leave you to choose a bed and settle in. Lunch won't be long, you can meet the others and then we'll get you started after that."

I was left alone in the huge echoing shed with its clinically cool whitewashed walls and the hint of uniform about the beds; the same white sheets, the same navy blankets, the same navy towels laid in the same way on each bed, a small rectangle window above each apartment allowing just enough light to cause dusky shadows to fall across the floor although it was just approaching midday.

How fine the distinction between practicality and institution can be? Will and Nicky's farm oozed warmth and community, bringing strangers together with a sense of purpose and family. A similar set up in my life would try to define me as a third class citizen with varying degrees of mental illness.

I swung my bag onto the top bed of the compartment at the end furthest from the toilets and showers, heaved myself up the sturdy wooden ladder and lay on my bed for a few minutes. I scanned the white corrugated roof, the corners and the entire compartment from the height of my bed and could see no sign of any cameras or listening devices, my chest easing a little at this reassurance. I dug into my bag and found the tape at the bottom, to check that it was still there. I had not yet decided how to deal with it but had taken the view that perhaps Stanley would have some suggestions. Now that I was in his locality, all I had to so was find him although with only one day off a week, I would not be successful quickly, if in fact he was still here.

An examination of my life illustrates how early I appeared to differ from my peers. At the hospital they keep suggesting that I suffer with some form of dementia; that such an illness may be hereditary as my paternal grandmother was heavily involved in the Poll Tax Riots, demonstrating a willingness to disbelieve and question the Government.

That silver haired lady with magical sparkling eyes died as I approached my sixth birthday, becoming the last of my grandparents to pass away. I spent a lot of time with her; whilst my father worked and my mother needed space and time to complete her chores at home, twice a week my grandmother would take me to the park where we would sit on a bench near the clear, bubbling river. The ducks would waddle playfully, hoping for the breadcrumbs that my grandmother would always have in her antique red carpet bag, which was crammed full with her knitting, sewing and address book. But lurking at the bottom of the bag was always something for me. It might be sweets or a toy but on my favourite occasions it would be a book from which my grandmother would read passages to me in the sweet, colourful lilt of her narration. Detailed, vivid images were brought to energetic life in my young mind by the words on the pages, aided by the beautifully intricate pictures and illustrations that my grandmother would present to me.

"Can you see it Fenn? Is the picture there, the boy in his car?" she would ask me, prompting the images and I would either nod or screw my eyes closed harder, willing the little boy to walk on to the screen in my head.
"I can see it Grandma, I can, I can!" I shrieked as I swung my legs excitedly.
"Okay, what's he wearing?"
"A red jumper and a blue pointy hat".
"Very good, what's his face like?"
"He's smiling, laughing. He's getting out of the car, ooh! He has a ball. A big green one. Now his friend has arrived."
"What's the friend wearing?"
"A green shirt and yellow shorts. They're throwing the ball to each other. Oh no! The friend won't give the ball back."

"How does the little boy feel?"

"He's sad and angry because it's his ball. He's telling his friend but his friend won't listen." I still had my eyes closed, my story playing itself out in my mind. My grandmother went quiet and after a moment, I slowly opened one eye to peer up at her and to see that she was smiling widely down at me. Her lips pressed together firmly, her head cocked to one side and her eyes shining brightly through glistening tears of pride that would not fall.

Hours were spent like that before my grandmother would wisely and quietly tell me that it was time to go home and take my hand whilst I would complain loudly that I didn't want to go home because no one read stories at home to me and that I wanted to know what happened next to Alice or Piggy or Bilbo.

"Grandma?"

"Yes, my darling?"

"How come the only books we have at my house are the ones with numbers and boring long words?"

"Don't you have any picture books?"

"No, only the ones I get from school."

My grandmother responded with a loud snort. She drew herself inwards and upwards and turned to face me.

"What does Daddy tell you?"

"He doesn't say anything but Mummy says that the books from school should be good enough."

I chattered loudly as I gambolled next to, behind, around and in front of my grandmother, blonde pigtails flapping around like lamb's tails.

"And what do you think?"

"I think they're boring and dull and all the same. Storytime at school isn't like reading stories with you. We have adventures."

My grandmother stopped and crouched down to take my hands in her hers and look deeply into my eyes.

"Well my darling, as long as you know what you do like and don't like, you won't go far wrong." I was standing stock still and nodded solemnly at her words to let her know that I understood.

But wander home we inevitably would, often to find my mother watching a documentary on television, or perhaps even dozing on the sofa before waking with a quick and awkward jerk. She would ask what we had been doing, so my grandmother would evasively summarise our afternoon, never directly referring to either the fact that we were reading or to what we were reading and it seemed that it would satisfy my mother who would offer my grandmother a cup of tea for the road. On one of the last occasions I remember before my grandmother's death, I was sat on the bench next to my grandmother eating a piece of chocolate cake- and making a proper mess of it- swinging my welly-clad legs care freely, whilst my mother and grandmother dipped their biscuits into their tea. We had been reading a book about a strange creature trekking through a fantasy world to destroy an evil ring, although I hadn't yet learned to appreciate the distinction between fact and fiction. (Father Christmas still worked as an effective form of inducement for good behaviour.) As I prepared to take another huge chunk from my cake and through the crumbled remains of the previous mouthful, I loudly asked my mother whether she had ever seen a dwarf. My mother's eyebrow arched severely, her brow furrowed deeply, expressions of her extreme displeasure as she sat opposite and stared directly at my grandmother who obdurately refused to look away and admit any wrongdoing.

"Where did you hear that word?" My mother's question was unequivocal, aimed unquestioningly at my grandmother rather than me; nevertheless she still fixed me in the powerful beam of her searching green eyes. The remains of the moist chocolate cake clung messily to my clumsy fingers, demanding my attention in full, while I avoided the intense gaze that my mother bore into me. I shrugged my shoulders, painfully aware of the conflict asserting itself between my mother and my grandmother. With unusually good timing and having had what seemed to be an exceptionally good day at the office, my father bounded into the kitchen, bursting through the door with jovial energetic enthusiasm. The issue of the dwarf was killed immediately.

I was dragged from my reveries by the voices that were raised in the yard when a bell rang for lunch. Jumping down from my bed, the similarities to school were uncanny and I felt a moment's pang of nostalgia towards my friends and classmates as I joined the back of a gathering group to head towards the packing shed. Although lunch was simple with soup, sandwiches, fruit and milk, it was jolly with a low buzz of chatter reverberating around the shed, along the lines of tables and around the cool concrete walls.

The others seemed a lot older than me, talking about university classes, offering opinions on different text books, schools of thought, tutors they rated highly, students they didn't. I had little to contribute to the conversation even if I had wanted to do so, so I maintained my silence and ate my lunch quietly and slowly whilst I snatched occasional glances at the group.

There were eleven of them; seven lads, four girls. They all seemed to know each other well, referring to the occurrences of last summer. In the midst of the group was a tall, broad shouldered man, whose hair was as dark as chocolate with eyes that shimmered in a deep emerald colour. He was sitting back, slightly slouched on the bench but his eyes, brightly alert, betrayed his attempted appearance of lethargy. Without moving the rest of his face, he winked at me, briefly but surely, and I allowed him a glancing smile before cowering back again over my lunch.

The bell sang out again and everyone gathered up the plates, glasses and rubbish, left them on a trolley at the end of the tables and headed off back into the fields. Bored of being on my own and eager to start work, I cautiously followed a few steps behind them out into the mesmerising sunshine.

I still miss the sanctuary of the orchards on the Farm; they were peaceful, quiet, an entire universe away from what seemed to be my fate as the trees protected us from the often intense heat of the sun, absorbing the cruel cut of the frequently brutal winds and beating back the power of the driving rain, kept our secrets and willingly gave up their fruits to us. The President shouldn't have worried about the Press, those orchards were plentiful, bearing witness to our discussions, debates and disputes. Every tree I approached I scoured carefully for any sign that the President's Agents had left their mark, but I saw none. To this day, I believe, one of the only things I believe in with all of my being, was the safety of the orchards. Yes, I have doubted my own innocence, but such doubts come, go, surface and appear again and again.

For the next few days, things didn't change in that I dutifully followed the routine, worked steadily and diligently and kept my own counsel. However, I started to allow myself giggles when others in the work force made jokes or performed something comical, I started to say hello and smile at breakfast lunch and dinner. I think the others thought I was shy and young; correct on the second count as I was only approaching my sixteenth birthday.

One evening, we had finished packing the fruit and were all vociferously ravenous, heading to the trough for dinner when the green-eyed guy spoke directly to me.
"So, come on then, what's your name?" It was a jovial enquiry.
"Louisa."
"Hi, Louisa, I'm Ben. Nice to meet you. Having fun?"
"Yeah, it's cool." I tried to sound nonchalant.
"Why don't you eat with us? I'll introduce you to everyone."
I shrugged my shoulders non-committedly and followed him to the benches.
"Guys, this is Louisa." There was a cacophony of hello's, hi's and nice to meet you's.
"This is Tim, Sarah, Kate, Paul, Rich, Vicky, Laura, Sam, Alex and Dave. C'mon sit!" he encouraged me as he spotted my shy reluctance, his energy and enthusiasm infectious. I clambered awkwardly over the bench to sit beside Ben, next to Dave and opposite Vicky, hoping desperately that I didn't

look as out of my depth as I felt.

"Are you having fun?" Vicky asked me.

"Yip. It's pretty cool, you know, how they just let us get on with it." I replied.

"It is. Unusual though. This is our fifth summer here. We all started together and keep coming back like a holiday of sorts, except we get paid!" She laughed.

"Wow. What do you do normally?"

"Well, we're all students of various guises. I'm studying engineering with Laura at Durham, Sam and Rich are reading law in London, Sarah's doing Physics at Oxford, really top end stuff, Vicky here is doing maths at Manchester, Paul is training to be a teacher, I think it's history, whatever that means, and Tim, Kate and Dave are working but studying computer science at night school." Alex sounded like a reporter.

"What about you?" I turned to look directly at Ben.

"I'm between jobs right now." He admitted but his eyes blazed with excitement; clearly lying but getting an extraordinary buzz from it, must be something secretive I thought. I looked at him carefully, he looked equally carefully at me and a flash of understanding dashed between us.

"And what do you do?" a cold chill swirled in my stomach as I performed the lie I had rehearsed in my head all morning.

"Just left school. Got bored, need a new challenge. So I'm travelling while I consider my options." I tried to sound casual and comfortable, like I knew what I was doing.

"Fair enough." I knew Ben had instantly recognised this as a lie, but I wasn't going to make it easy for him, however it appeared that Alex was satisfied with my answer.

"What was your old job then?" I asked Ben openly.

"Well, I was a student English teacher but I didn't like the way that we were being taught to teach. So I left." It was a succinct and brusque summary, failing to convince me that there wasn't anything more to the story. I probed further.

"And what are you doing now?"

Ben dropped his head towards me and shifted closer.

"I'm a writer."

My suspicions had been confirmed. Head bowed, reverently, I nodded to let him know that I understood the implications of his vocation and said no more whilst I helped myself to a brimming bowlful of the steaming meaty stew that Nicky had brought to the table.

We hung around in the packing shed after dinner for a while, the air previously warmed by the sunshine now dissipating quickly; they painted me a bold, vibrant picture of student life, working life and their plans for the future and in return I told them as little as possible. What I did tell them was mainly made up of superficial truths as I didn't think I would ever remember all the lies I would need to tell if everything I told them was false; seemingly irrelevant things like music I liked, authors I read and holidays I had been on, I didn't mention anyone I knew or had known, I wanted to leave no trace of my old self or life.

I still had no idea of who these people were or why they worked here each summer religiously; besides their stories what had I learned? Their motivations were anonymous at this stage, political persuasions as yet unexplained. Whilst I could keep myself to myself, eventually questions would be asked and I would be required to answer truthfully, lie or avoid the question and currently I did not possess the information to decide what to do. The ice cold thought that I might have to take a risk and the possible consequences of such risks terrified me; I was barely 16 years old and had no-one I could trust.

We went to bed an hour or so later and I wandered across the starlit yard to the dorm with Ben, lagging a little behind the others.
"I don't know what it is, but you can trust us. All of us." He whispered urgently but firmly, with a stern, earnest face.
"Ok." I shrugged his comment off as irrelevant and hadn't needed to be said but he grabbed my wrist quickly but tenderly, it made me spin and turn to face him squarely. His eyes fixed on mine intently.
"I mean it. Wait, let me just say this. When I said I was a

144

writer, I meant it, but not just a normal one. I write stuff about the President, the Government. We're all part of an underground thing, so we can help you."

I noticed that the strip light in the dormitory ahead buzzed loudly, the air was still thick and cloying and I didn't know how best to react, to protect myself. Could I really trust these people? I didn't know them even though I had been observing them, hoping I could.

"I know you've got a secret, it sets you apart from everyone else. I can see that you're lonely, that you need to tell someone else." His urgent whisper broke into a low gruff sound. On the edge of the darkness, on the border with the artificial light, I searched every feature, every crevice for the reassurance and help that I had craved since I had fled from Philip.

"Look it's late, I need to sleep." I resisted the pull of the temptation, there would be other chances to assess the situation. Ben let my wrist slip away from his grasp.

"Ok, I didn't mean to scare you, I just want you to know that I do understand and want to help. Sleep well, I'll still be here tomorrow as will the others."

I relaxed slightly, he wasn't angry with me but accepted that I needed to think about what he'd said. He'd trusted me with his desperately important secret, one that was not only his but the whole group, and now I didn't know if he would now expect the same from me, or whether this was a trap? A sharp pain stabbed at the front my head as I laid down on to the cool firmness, I didn't know what to do, but my confusion seemed an effective sedative as I fell into the oblivion of asleep deeply and quickly.

The next fortnight passed peacefully and busily, Ben was still friendly, nothing had changed, but he didn't mention to me anything again. A day off was coming up and I told Nicky I wanted to go into town. She said that the others were going and was sure they wouldn't mind me tagging along. I was slightly disappointed that they hadn't mentioned it but when I spoke to Vicky, during the afternoon in the Orchards, she welcomed me and said that she was sorry that they no-one had said anything, it had slipped her mind and was sure it was the same for the others. I was slightly appeased.

"What are you going to get up to?" She enquired.
"I thought I might go to the hairdressers, haven't been for ages."
"You needn't bother spending money on that, I can cut hair, I used to do it as a Saturday job. I'll get my scissors out after dinner tonight if you like?" She offered enthusiastically.
"That'd be great. I could do with saving the money but only if you're sure." I enthused reciprocally.
"Of course I am. Think about what kind of style you want."
I didn't need to, I knew what was needed.

We finished dinner a little later than usual as a result of the larger than normal pick we had gathered, and I left with Vicky to the dormitory; she sat me on a stool and stood with scissors at the ready.

"Ok, take it all off." I said.

"Are you sure? Your hair is way past your shoulders blades, it's beautifully fine, there's lots of it and will take ages to grow back." She protested animatedly and knowledgably.

"Yes, I'm sure." I said firmly.

Vicky stared cutting with a steady hand and was about three quarters of the way finished, when we heard a screech of tyres in the court yard. I caught a flash of black and yellow in the mirror and in the moment that Vicky had turned away to see what was going on I had dived under the bed with my head flat to the hard cold concrete floor and my back pressed to the wall I listened to the loud but indistinct voices, sharp footsteps on the concrete yard, more voices further away, the slam of car doors and the grind of tyres moving off again. From the darkest corner I could see the door being gently pulled shut and I slid out. Vicky stood there, scissors still in one hand, a lock of her own in the other.

"They saw the hair on the floor. I had to pretend I was cutting my own. Thankfully our hair colour is a similar shade of blonde." She explained softly. "You can tell me if you want to but I do need to finish your hair to stop you looking silly." She giggled.

We remained silent while I sat still to let her finish cutting, but I couldn't hide my violent trembling, pronounced goose bumps and uncontrollable shivering no matter what I tried to think about. After what seemed like an hour Vicky finished and paraded my new elfin crop in front of the mirror. It was completely different. I almost didn't recognise myself and slowly the tears came, trickling slowly over across the dark shadows under my eyes, cutting pathways over my dusty cheeks.

"I just don't know who to trust." I muttered my admission weakly.

"I don't have any magic words to make you believe me or trust us but I'll try to explain who we are. You can then decide." She suggested. I nodded.

"We all met as cadets in the Presidential Academy, a decade ago. We were the young bright things of our intake. He wanted to parade us as models for the rest of the youth, but we realised what was happening when we saw colleagues disappear, never heard from again. Unfortunately we couldn't leave before we had graduated, because to have done so would have raised questions and drawn attention to the fact that we thought and had opinions and views that differed so badly from the rest. So when we graduated none of us accepted the jobs they offered us; job security they said but it sounded like a ridiculous misnomer to us. We all went to our different universities, chose our respective courses and began to live our lives like the rest of you all. However, we couldn't forget what we had seen and heard, the statements drilled into us and the feeling that this wasn't quite natural. At the end of the first year, we saw the advert for this place and thought it would be a fantastic chance to catch up again. But by the time we met up, we'd had almost a year apart and all the first week we argued and bickered.

We were so confused and bewildered, for one we couldn't understand what had happened. All eleven of us had been so close through academy and now we couldn't spend an hour together without a cross word. When we finally admitted that there was a problem, we all said "You've all changed" which was true but so had we all. We eventually appreciated for the first time our individuality and the fact that we had all formed our own views of life, but that those views weren't right or wrong, just collated from our different experiences. As soon as we recognised this life became a lot easier, we then enjoyed debating with each other, learning from each other because we all had jokes, stories and wisdom to impart and learn.

Then we started to break down and analyse the institutionalised education that we had received, to consider what we'd been taught and why. We questioned the methods of the President and the Government. And our conclusions? That the President is desperate to hang onto power any way he can. His primary method is by restricting free thought and speech, for example schools are told what they cannot teach to their pupils and last year a law was passed without the public knowing, creating a criminal offence of causing harm by using offensive, dangerous or provocative language. You'll have to ask Rich or Sam about the specifics but they say it is a really wide law with serious consequences.

We're all actively involved in the underground movement which is trying to open people's minds to bring awareness of this mass manipulation. It's becoming like guerrilla warfare, we've all see friends picked off by the Presidential Guard, but we know how important this is- our ability for rational free thought, independent speech is what marks humans out, if we lose it, we might as well go out and graze in the fields."

Her face was grim, set with her teeth clenched and her jaw hard. I felt I was being examined by her intense, startling blue eyes; that she was waiting for me. A strange sense of relief passed over me as I made the decision and let my story pour forth to the passively receptive Vicky who did not interrupt, did not question me but simply sat on the edge of the bed and keenly listened. I paced the floor with anger as I told the story, violently dropped my hands as I vented my thoughts and suspicions and released my fears whilst dragging my hands over the hair that was no longer there. I felt no need to persuade, cajole or justify the truth of my story to Vicky. She seemed to absorb it unquestioningly, almost like she had been expecting it. I finished with an explanation about my suspicions of Ben. On the only occasion in which must have been an hour, she laughed.

"You've got to be joking!" She blurted out and seeing the weird expression on my face continued quickly. "No, wait let me explain. Ben's family disappeared. About three years ago? It was in the newspapers, his aunt informed on them. His parents and elder sister were dragged screaming from the house. He was playing with a friend at a neighbour's house and saw the whole thing through their bedroom window. He was about, what, five? When his aunt realised he hadn't been taken, she sent him to the Academy. I think she felt so guilty when she realised how far the Presidential Guard went and thought he would be safe. You won't find anyone who feels as strongly about this as Ben. It's so personal for him."

Visions in my head flicked to the farm and the devastated house, lives torn apart by the sheer thuggery of it all. There was no direct link between the two but the vicious assaults on two separate families were tragically familiar. An overwhelming sadness enveloped me in a heavy, dense blanket, my eyes began to water, partly with exhaustion and strangely from the relief of finally sharing my burden with someone.

"Look, get some sleep. It's really late. I'll speak to the others and see what they know or think. I'm sure we'll find Stanley." Vicky's words soothed my aching head.

That night I slept so soundly I finally realised how proper sleep felt, despite a dull glow in my stomach reminding me that my future was in their hands.

The sun rose bright and warm, light squeezing as hard as it could through the small windows to flood the dorm with yellow so that I could tell immediately it was a beautiful, cloudless sky before I even opened my eyes.

The others were already in the Orchard by the time I'd even got to breakfast, Nicky told me that they'd let me sleep because they were worried. She asked me if I was alright and when I reassured her that I was, she said I was free to go out to the Orchard when I was ready. As I approached the picking patch I could tell that there was something wrong. It was quiet, without any laughter, sombre, I could hear no banter, heads were down. Eventually, Vicky caught my eye as I sauntered down the avenue of fruit trees.

"Hi, how are you doing? Sleep well eh?" She was over enthusiastic, trying hard, a big false grin spread across her face as she bounded up to me, almost Labrador like.

"I'm good, can't believe I slept so well?" I said brightly. "How's picking?"

"Great. Most of these are ready to be picked. Not like yesterday." Alex chipped in.

"Cool, I best get started then." I turned to pull gently at a delicate peach with its velvet fur sparkling with the lingering early morning dew.

The morning passed eventually, and while it did I worked out that whatever had happened had created a rift in the group between Vicky and Ben on the one side and Tim and Kate on the other side of what I could perceive was an ever deepening void. Where everyone else fitted into this uncomfortable picture, I could not tell. Vicky's blue eyes were as intense as ever but now so powerfully piercing, I felt I was going to be cut by a laser when she looked at me.

Time crawled by was we struggled towards lunch, but eventually it arrived and we traipsed down the picking avenue back to the packing shed. Ben unsubtly and tactlessly dropped his glove right in front of me.

"Hi, how are things?" He grinned, lifting his head as he extended upwards from the ground. There was an even louder obvious "tut" as Kate walked past, her glare burning into mine so hard I had to look away in obvious discomfort.

"What's going on?" I demanded so less subtly than either Kate or Ben had been that it caused them all to look around sharply. I had had enough of whatever childish petulance was going on. Perhaps I was more disappointed that these people who I had perceived to be mature hadn't really grown up at all, they were no better than the girls at St Catherine's. Kate rolled her eyes, kept walking and I heard Tim clearly mutter something about making a fuss, whether about me or Kate I couldn't distinguish, and at that point, could not have cared less.

"Oh bollocks to this. Look, on Sunday we're all going into town to meet some mates. People who've had not dissimilar experiences to you and I. I want you to come."

"But the others don't?" I surmised quickly.

"They don't share my view but that's what all this is about isn't it?" The slight flush in his cheeks spoiled his succinct diplomacy. "Look, they think you're too young and feel that they don't really know you. Yeah, I know Vicky explained to them what you had told her but it seems too convenient to them. To Vicky, Alex and I it makes complete sense. Look, some pretty interesting people come to this meeting, they might be able to help you."

"Why would I want to go to a meeting where, as far as I can

tell eight of the people attending this meeting don't want me to go?"

"This isn't about them. Look at the bigger picture. The underground network is pretty tight, we all know. Someone who knows Someone. Just think it over?"

I could not understand why he wanted me to go to this meeting so badly and the issue went round my head in a circular motion for the next day or so while Tim and Kate tried not to grimace so obviously at me and until suddenly it was Sunday morning.

Chapter 12

A beautiful clear day, clouds were nowhere to be seen and the sky almost shimmered like a swimming pool glistening in the sunshine. It was still early, we had just finished breakfast, but the heat was starting to build so that there as almost a tangible tension engulfing us, pressing against our skin that was still damp from our earlier showers. I hadn't thought about the meeting at all, I had decided immediately after my conversation with Ben that I would attend, that I wouldn't let Tim or Kate prevent me furthering my own ambitions, stopping me from doing what I knew was best and what I knew I ought to do. I just didn't tell Ben.

His face lit up like a beacon when he realised that I had

climbed into Nicky's MPV after him.

"Fantastic!" He exclaimed loudly and pointedly.

Tim and Kate smiled painfully and shrank into the corner, I hadn't seen what I'd seen to care about they thought and to hide from what was the right thing to do.

"So, let's go!" I countered and the vehicle screeched out of the yard, jerking me back onto the seat.

What had seemed to take me hours to walk, weeks ago previously, took us a little over ten minutes to drive. A silent ten minutes but it passed quickly enough and soon the suburban surroundings eased into familiarity in a faint ghostly way. Nicky drew the MPV to a halt in the town square just off the main high street, jumped out and released us from the back.

"Right, I'll pick you up at 5pm. Anyone late has to walk and it's going to be cold after dark tonight." She spoke softly but sternly to us all, her eyes not leaving Ben. "Look after each other." her voice dropped off as she eased the car away on to the grey tarmac that stretched away into the distance.

"C'mon, this way!" Ben took the lead.

We all walked together as a small band for twenty minutes or so through the town centre. It was quiet, some older residents were pottering in and out of the antique shops, and others sat at the wooden benches in beer gardens, enjoying the sunshine. We chatted about work and the weather, until we came to a huge playing field. At the far end was some children's play equipment, slides, swings, climbing frames. The rest of the field was abandoned to the vivid lush green grass on which a few lads were playing football. They were being watched by two girls and another boy who's closely shaved pale blond hair was strikingly similar to something deep in my recollections that I couldn't yet reach despite the distance of field that we still had to cross. His bony shoulders protruded uncomfortably through the thin navy blue t-shirt that didn't quite hide the waistband of his red tartan boxer shorts as he sat cross legged on the grass, his bony fingers plucking at the grass as if it were a musical instrument. A bit confused and a bit more surprised, I followed the others heading towards this group. Paul, Rich and Alex joined the footballers, the rest of us sat on the grass with the two girls and the boy, who looked up, right at me and then it hit me.

It hit me hard, in the ribs, a tight constrained feeling enveloped me, I couldn't move. I couldn't breathe. I just stared.

"This is Louisa, Jim." Ben's voice broke the block that had frozen me entirely.
"Louisa, hi. Nice to meet you." He nodded slightly with the most subtle flick of an eyelid. The tension that was warping my

whole body eased slightly. "So how's things Ben? Can't believe it's been a year!"

"I know it's flown by. Still trying to write?"

"Yeah, managed to get some stuff out to the US. Used a web café down south about two months ago, whilst I was working in this book shop. The owner was half Greek- a really good bloke- and he had good contacts across Europe, introduced me to a few of them. Those who could smuggle stuff out. Really dangerous but it is good to know that there is an outlet."

"Aren't you taking a few too many risks?" Vicky asked.

"I guess I am, but it's indicative of how desperate we've become. I'm hoping that these are educated gambles."

Stanley's gaze scanned the shade of the trees that lined the field, in the distance gold shafts of sunlight filtered through the canopy of leaves. Deep amongst the murky shadows, the rays tumbled off the leaves and bounced off something onto the ground, throwing sparks into the air which glistened in the bright sunshine. The sparks trapped Jim's/Stanley's attention for a moment, his brow furrowed and his eyes focused on whatever lurked beneath the trees. One of the guys playing football caught sight of Stanley's uncomfortable paranoid and headed into the woods, chasing down a well-aimed pass of the football to investigate. The source of this minor panic turned out to be a crisp packet, which was then carefully examined for any sign of espionage. When none was found, the release from the tension was almost tangible so as to lead to complacent relaxation. I couldn't let them wallow in any false perceptions.

"They know you're here y'know." I croaked, my nerves stifled my voice.
"Sorry?" He seemed slightly taken aback at my impertinence.
"They know you are here." I repeated, my voice gathering strength, more confident of what I knew.
"How do you know that?"

I explained my mother's role, who she was and what I'd seen. I set out in detail the surveillance techniques used by my mother's staff, like the cameras and microphones concealed in common place, unremarkable objects and places. I described the video footage I had been shown, demonstrating that no-one could be trusted in view of the use of observation agents by the President. In turn they asked questions of me- how I knew the things I did, why I was disclosing this- and with Vicky's prompting and assurances I told them everything including my motivations, almost laying myself open whilst the small band listened with earnest attention. I forgot where I was and the circumstances in which I found myself; the intense suspicion and crippling paranoia seemed to dwindle slightly.
"So you're not Louisa?" Stanley spoke clearly and scepticism in his voice alarmed me.

"Huh? Don't you believe me?"

"Frankly I don't know and that is irrelevant. Quite clearly, you're not Louisa. And you need to leave here now." He said firmly.

"No! Why?" Ben protested on my behalf.

Stanley, Jim, whoever he wanted to be, threw a newspaper into Ben's lap and stalked away.

"Got to go guys! Sorry, something has come up. See you soon!" He called gaily.

For the second time inside five minutes I felt like I'd been hit by lightning, frozen to the spot, couldn't move, couldn't speak. The help and solace that I was desperately seeking seemed to ebb into the hazy sunshine away from my scrambling mind.

Ben was frantically scanning the newspaper. What could it be? Eventually, he finished, looked far into the distance for a moment and then manoeuvred himself closer to me.

"Try to look relaxed, like we're just any group of friends meeting up." He whispered, his head hung low but glancing at me, like those movie stars did in films my mother had liked. I played my part, lifted my head and giggled because I understood what I needed to do.

"Good girl. Wait a bit before reading this." He beamed at me as he gave me a nudge with his shoulder to which I responded with a shove. We carried on for a while joking, playing and flirting (I almost enjoyed myself) so that I ended up lying up on my front, feet pulled up into the air. At this point I decided that I could get away with reading the paper, I pressed it flat to the grass so that anyone watching from a distance could not tell what I was reading. To assist the charade, Vicky threw me a book she'd had in her bag.

With a trepidation that gripped my whole body, I unfolded the paper and struggled to suppress the small gasp that escaped me as I came face to face with the old me.

A saccharine smile revealed my milky white teeth; carefree and immaculate but spoiled all the same as half of the page was filled with my last school photograph, my long blonde hair spread across my shoulders, school uniform neatly in place. The detailed piece set out the story of my life so far with a few embellishments and half-truths, such as the assumption that I had been kidnapped because of my mother's position. Emblazoned across the top of the page were the figures £500,000, whilst the story detailed the precise conditions of the reward. I flicked through the rest of the paper and I noticed a small article describing a speech made to a conference of Presidential Guards by a spokesperson from the President's Office in which the Guards were urged to use their eyes and ears to enforce every law on the statute book, serving justice would be their reward together with the grateful thanks of the ignorant nation as a whole. The speech had applauded various individual guards who had apprehended numerous enemies of the state, such persons who had betrayed their status as citizens, used weapons of the mind against innocent citizens and had subverted the true and proper causes of the state. The good deeds should continue, the writer concluded.

I turned back to the front page which confirmed my suspicion; at the bottom of the article about me was a reference to the article. The connection between them did not seem to be just arbitrary or random; I knew there was a reason. An epiphany of awareness struck me; I was wanted by the State in connection with my father's death. The ruse that I had been kidnapped was to arouse public sympathy to make members of the public even more willing to turn me in, along with a reward with possibly further rewards of citizenship and nationwide fame. From the time that the writer had got the information from the Government I had now become a highly valuable object and saw exactly why Stanley didn't want me hanging around. Their group was based on trust and the bounty on my head would corrupt the group, becoming a corrosive force affecting their way of thinking, dividing their unity and distracting them from their true work.

"I'm going to have to go." I spoke clearly and firmly. "Mum's needs me back." Ben nodded, he understood, there would be people like Tim and Kate who I couldn't trust. He glanced at

Vicky.

"Before you do. We need to know something." she said.

"Ok."

"You seem to be the only person we know to have seen what you've seen, you know the cameras and the files." he dropped his voice to barely a murmur.

"if you say so,"

"How did you get in?" Vicky was almost amazed.

"With an identity card, it swiped me through every gate. My mother had it arranged for me."

"You've not still got it?"

"Um, oooh, yeah! It's still in my wallet." I dug out my wallet and flicked through it until I found it; still pristine with my photograph, name and user number.

"Here you go. I don't know how much use it'll be, as it's probably been wiped and if it hasn't they'll be on the look out for me."

"Fantastic, don't worry, our expert computer hackers will find this perfect." Ben's face was aglow with excitement.

"Well, I'll start walking back now and grab my stuff. Best I get out of here sooner rather than later." I got up slowly, faced up to Ben, Vicky and Alex who had jogged over from the football whilst Ben and I had been talking. With a shrug of my shoulders, I engaged in their embraces and said goodbye before I began to meander back across the field. I hadn't noticed how long the grass had been as I reached the edge and looked back with a surprising fondness - I'd only known them all a couple of weeks- I could barely see their heads above the grass where they had sat back down, reclining back on their elbows.

My walk back to the Farm was without hurry, at a leisurely pace and I used the time to consider my options. The money I had earned over the past few weeks was still whole. I hadn't really spent anything and at this point in my life it seemed a considerable amount and meant I had options.

The first option was to leave the country. Where? The US had severed all links with us since the President had refused to repeal the "Protection of Power" Legislation. The US had used aggressive human rights rhetoric, had threatened boycotts and sanctions but then simply ignored us when our President boldly announced to the world that we would defend ourselves at all cost and made it clear in the plainest language that no one should be in any doubt as to our nuclear capabilities. The US publicly took the view that we would need their economic support more than they really wanted to enforce UN policy by force and so they had withdrawn all trade and stuck us on their blacklist, wouldn't trade anything not even allow individuals onto planes heading that way from the continent. I didn't have to go to the US but the problem was lot of other countries had followed the US example.

And then there was the difficulty of the passport, even if I had had it with me, I could not have used it. Everyone who could read or watch a television or radio probably now knew my name and face, greedy minds guarding my precious image from the loss of the highly prized reward offered by my would-be captors. I could not remember when a reward at all was offered let alone such a high one as people were generally pleased enough with the prizes of citizenship and recognition, but this was a risky tactic. If people found out that I had not been kidnapped what would their reaction be? I suppose if I admitted being an alleged criminal I would attract far less sympathy and they would probably turn me in anyway. It was likely that no-one would believe the truth; I was now walking away from the only people who accepted my version of events.

I reached this lonely conclusion just as I reached the Farm from where loud voices were being exchanged. I hid behind the packing shed perched at the edge so that I could hear.
"Is she here? Tell me the truth!" The man's voice was cold, I recognised it immediately and my stomached lurched forward, taking me with it. I stretched my hand out against the rough, stone wall to balance me but my arm trembled against my weight.

"No, she is not here." Nicky's voice was weak, pitiful and resigned.

"Have you seen her?" He demanded.

"Yes" she whispered.

"When and where?"

"Earlier today, she went into town."

"Where?"

"I don't know."

There was a dull thud. What had I done? I peered around the corner, two ape-like Presidential Guards had their backs to me, I could see Nicky slumped against the wall of the house, legs spread awkwardly, almost crumpled underneath her, I don't know what shocked me more; the sight of her face- swollen, bloody and beaten- or the fact that she was naked. I didn't need to look twice at Will to see that he was dead without any sign of beating, which surprised me. I caught a terrible glimpse of the tortured tragedy in Nicky's eyes, as though a fire burned within, the pain seemed to seer though her. A cold breeze whipped me across the face.

"Where did she go?"

"I don't know." Nicky screamed with defiant honesty, electricity coursed through me, she thrust herself forward to face her assailant, and with the most bravery I have ever seen of anyone, she let go her last breath. She pulled herself up the wall, only she and the Presidential Guard would ever know what had happened although from the giveaway places of horrifying vivid grazes, cuts and bruises I could only guess there could be only one repulsive conclusion.

The same voice laughed with icy cruelty.

"I don't care, we'll find her anyway." and with that he pulled his trigger and Nicky collapsed to the ground. A trickle of blood slowly leaked from the small neat hole in Nicky's forehead.
"Do what you want with the bodies." he said contemptuously and dismissively to his underlings and stalked away alarmingly in my direction.

Stunned, I forced myself to pad silently along the back wall of the packing shed to the house and through the back door. It was utter carnage; the beasts had not only violated Nicky but had desecrated the house too. I crawled into the cupboard under the stairs in the hallway and nestled at the back of the dark hole, underneath the lowest steps, among some old blankets.

I remained frozen, paralysed with fear until the coolness of dusk arrived and I began to collect myself to move on. As I got to the front of the house, the phone rang. The blinking red light on the front of the machine told me that another message had already been left. "Nicky? Will? It's Ben, where are you? What's happened?"

Instinctively, I dashed back and snatched up the phone.

"It's me! They've been here, they're dead. It's a mess! I'm so sorry."

"Get off the line" Stay where you are! We'll walk!" The line went dead.

I crept up the stairs and found an airing cupboard for sanctuary. As I passed the windows, I could see a smouldering pyre; echoes of the previous farm deafened me. What was I doing to people? Why did they want me so badly? How could I stop this? I pondered the only answer I could find, my whole being sank into the pile of duvets, towels and bed sheets, and sleep swept over me.

Chapter 13

It was dark when muffled voices stirred me and I edged open the door to recognise Ben's low urgent whisper, as I peered through the banister railings following the comfort of his voice. The stairs creaked lazily as he firmly placed a foot on the first step, I watched shadows dance across his face as the pyre continued to burn and he climbed the stairs slowly.

"Hi" I croaked. His head whipped round to see me crouched against the rails.

"Fenn" He breathed my name and rushed forward. To hear my

real name released a wave of relief, as I let him pick me up from the floor, pull me to him and held me to his chest. "What happened?"

Tiredness seemed to percolate from me; tears slowly seeped down my cheeks.

"I came back and they were here. Will was already dead, they'd shot him through the head. Nicky was naked, beaten badly, I think they did other stuff before I got here, they had her at gun point, all she said was that I had been here, she wouldn't say where I had gone. They know I've been here. I think she saw me but still didn't say anything, so they shot her. I was hiding downstairs until you phoned." I rapidly stammered through my hurried synopsis of events and was taken aback by the firm, tender but warm embrace with which I was grasped by Ben.
"Look guys, we need to leave now. The van is in the garage, got a full tank from what I can see. The bastards have cut the electricity and water, I think they were expecting you to return here. They might be watching. Where's the rest of your stuff? Still in the dorm? I'll see what I can do." Lightly and smoothly but effortlessly and quickly, Alex almost galloped back down the stairs; professional calm and efficient.
"He's right, c'mon let's go." Ben released me and dragged me by the arm. He gathered my pack to head downstairs and I

meekly followed. I was beyond tired, a weary resignation had set in, accepting that I would be captured no matter where I went. Ben, however was not ready to surrender.

"C'mon!" He urged. "This isn't over." He yanked me after him and I broke free from my limp surrender as I landed hard at the bottom of the stairs, my knees buckling slightly at the impact.

We raced out of the front door, across the yard, into the garage. Alex had got the MPV started and was ready to go.

"OK! GO!" Ben urged. Alex jammed his foot onto the accelerator and the van squealed away from the garage.

"Wait, where are the others?"

"On the way, we'll pick them up on the road." He drove the vehicle hard out of the yard, down the track back towards the road. No sign of anyone on the road. It was empty, desolate, lit only by the harsh glare of the moon in a cold cloudless sky, it seemed alien with a stillness I have never experienced before or since. I wondered if the President was now able to control nature now?

The stillness was alarming. My hands gripped the back of the seat, my knees dug into the sponge of the seat back and I scanned the darkness, through the clouds of dust thrown up by the speeding van. As the van careered along, rocking violently from side to side, the stars blurred, so that all I could see was black.

"Where are they?" Alex demanded.

"I don't know, I didn't see them." Ben replied, his hands tearing at his hair.

"Well we can't go back." Alex decided.

"They'll be alright, won't they?" I asked.

A harsh suffocating silence filled the van, it was airless, uncomfortable, despite the air rushing through the open window into the cavernous van.

Alex kept the van at its top speed for half an hour until we met the by-pass, which was deserted and he brought the van to a more normal pace.

"We need to get off the road, ditch the van and regroup as soon as possible." Ben talked to himself as much as to us- he needed to form a plan of action.

"Um, I think I know where we can go. It's about twenty minutes from here; it's on the other side of town."

"Will they know about it? Will it be safe?" Alex asked me.

"Yes, and as much as anywhere else right now. I reckon we'll get away with it because they've been there one before. They took what they wanted and left it ruined." My voice shook with uncertainty. From now on every decision could have dire consequences and I wasn't sure I was ready for that responsibility.

After half an hour of careful driving and constant observation under the orange glow of the street lights, we reached the farm track. Alex switched off the headlights as soon as we were off the main road and let the van creep into the farm yard. Nothing seemed obviously out of place from when I had left it so many weeks before.

I led Alex and Ben stealthily through the house, almost like some morbid ghost walk, I showed them my gruesome discoveries. Carefully and deliberately, we checked each and every room of all of the buildings, satisfying ourselves as best as we could that no one was lurking, waiting to ambush us again.

"Right guys, get behind the van and push- we need to get it out of sight as far as we can." Alex practically dragged me out of the house, my legs shaking with adrenaline. When we had finished, the van was stuffed into a ditch between two fields, hidden by thick stuffy hawthorn hedges. Ben grabbed my backpack before we abandoned the vehicle and carried it back to the house.

"First light, I'll get the wheel back on that landrover and give it a once over. With a bit of luck, we can use that." Alex though aloud. "But let's get some sleep."
"Before we do, I've got something to show you. It's really

important." I stuttered as I stumbled back towards the house.

Both of the lads raised their eyebrows as I rooted through the stuffy to find the answerphone machine. My stomach flipped over and I retched again as the tape played its terrible story. The horror on Ben's face was too much and I ran to the bathroom to vomit. Alex was stonily faced and his face set hard as he realised the importance of the tape and the need to protect it at all costs.

"Oh fuck." He broke the silence. "This is unbelievable. It is the evidence that the international community needs to understand what is going on." He looked intently at Ben.
"Absolutely, how do we get it out?"
"Well, god, who do we trust that has the most contacts?"
Alex pulled at his hair madly. I wrapped my arms around my body as the adrenaline leaked from me and the cold night air seeped into my bones as Ben and Alex discussed their contacts.
"Let's sleep on it and not make any rash decisions. It's vital we get this right." Alex nodded at Ben's suggestion, one eye on me.

We climbed the stairs, one at a time until we reached the top rooms. It meant that we would hear anyone trying to get into the house and we climb out of the window as to the roof, to escape via a trellis that was attached to the wall at the end of the lower part of the roof. Everything we did now was done together and our first thought was always how to escape if we need to. We all slept in the same room; the boys gallantly gave me the bed and dragged in mattresses from the other rooms. We were going to stick together.

The fear and adrenaline had sapped all of my energy so that once I had lain down under the slightly stale duvet and my head on the damp pillow, my body shut down; my mind not long behind it.

Chapter 14

The warm sun glowed upon my eyelids; I felt the warmth as I began to stir. It was such a lovely way to wake that for a moment, I forgot the trauma of the night before. I seemed like a normal teenager for a split second and imagined my mother shouting at me to get up. But slowly my wits began to gather again and I reluctantly sat up in bed.

The boys had obviously woken earlier and had got up, leaving the duvets as they were- messy, body shaped cavities and all. Creeping slowly down the stairs, the birds were singing loudly outside and I found the boys with the landrover.
"Morning, sleepyhead! How you doing?" Alex grabbed me to

him, sideways; a streak of oil flashed across his forehead.

"I'm good- slept well." I said with a large yawn.

"Good stuff." Ben started yawning again. "Right, we're not sure it's good to hang around here for much longer. The Guard are bound to be searching everywhere for us. Alex, here, has got the landrover up and running, we've got a full tank and a spare of diesel. So, how about we head up further north towards Scotland?"

"Uh, my passport won't work." I said deflatedly.

"Ah ha! Ben has been a genius." Alex smiled broadly and handed me an A4 envelope. Rummaging inside I found a passport, driving licence and credit card, all in the name of Kathryn Walker. The first time I had seen her picture, I hadn't fully appreciated just how alike we looked. This unknown girl might just save my life.

After a sweep of the house to make absolutely sure that we would leave no trace of being there, putting all the beds back into perfect order and wiping away finger prints in the dust, Alex grabbed the maps that I had found in the office and we climbed into the aging green landrover.

Rain clouds started to gather as we trundled along the farm track, our bodies slamming against each other with the juddering from the terrain. We headed south for a few hours, sticking to the quieter A roads, avoiding motorways and anywhere there might be cameras like town centres. It was difficult, knowing that there were hidden cameras in unexpected places, to find places to get food and rest up safely. Eventually, Alex and Ben came up with a plan to get the tape out of the UK to the United States through someone called Lucy.

"Lucy is based in Edinburgh, works for one of the state publishing companies. You'll find her work in most schools, with the approval of the President, but she's our secret weapon. We don't think anyone suspects her, yet." Ben explained to me.

"We won't meet her directly, we'll catch up with other contacts and get the tape to her that way."

"Shouldn't we keep a copy? Just in case?" I suggested.

"That would be sensible." Alex looked at me approvingly. "Just a question of how. Any helps from Stan is out as he'll be even more heavily watched now, if he hasn't been arrested." My stomach lurched with guilt as Alex flipped on the radio, meaningless music was being aired so he turned the volume down.

"If something's happened, I'm sure we'll hear about it." Alex grimaced and Ben nodded.

We continued our journey south in silence but began to head east, towards the coast and away from the setting sun.

The melancholy setting of the sun brought a sadness and introspection that I hadn't experienced before. My birth was a direct result of the combination of science and unconditional, unlimited love. My parents had been trying for sometime to have a child but without fruition. It was never established what the difficulty was but the pinnacle of their hopes, dreams, indeed their lives, arrived in the form of me just after midnight on October 30. They had watched all the processes, spoken to all the scientists and asked every question they could think of from the make of the test tube to the exact chemistry involved in the conception. Nothing was too mundane for them and nothing was too much for them. Over a decade my father had established a successful accountancy practice, which wasn't anything big rather steady with reliable clients so that during their barren years my parents saved for the day that I would enter their lives. They weren't particularly frugal but neither were they luxuriously extravagant people.

Once they had decided that they wanted to try for children my mother volunteered to leave work to prepare. My mother was happy, glad to domestically support my father and keep their lives in a state of readiness for my arrival or for that matter, anyone's arrival. There had been others but none had managed to make it very far and each time they gave up to become another ghostly memory, my mother sank into a stifling, suffocating paralysis that shook my father to his core.

Having left for each potential glorious visit to the consultant, they would return to the house wrapped protectively in their private blanket of silence. What they didn't speak, the rest of the world didn't know, but could only guess as the taxi pulled up to the house. The net curtains around the cul-de-sac would twitch and the neighbours would murmur the prayers that my parents would never hear. The kettle would boil and the tea would cool, barely touched. My father would wander the empty, lifeless house looking for something that was not there but all the same aware of the shifting ghosts and my mother would lie huddled on the bed among the pillows and duvets that were bundled untidily beneath her, her hands twisting the corners of the duvet cover in her sorrow, tears staining the pillow and each one taking with it, its dues and tolls. The house would smell grey, feel dirty and while the lights were on they failed to penetrate the tense, desperate pleas emanating from the eerily silent rooms.

"You should rest." My father would blame my mother without knowing it.
"I don't need to" she would tersely respond and continue stirring her half mug of cold coffee aggressively.
"Your body is suffering, you should let it grieve and recover."
"And what about me?" She spat back.
"I am talking about you. You never sit still, you're always

running about, organising things, worrying about things and trying to do ten things at once."

"So what am I supposed to do?"

"You're supposed to let me help".

She let the words hit her in the stomach, along with so much pain that she'd already felt, the words sank into the depths after swirling around for a moment. My father then would listen to the silent resentment radiating from my mother. Her blank eyes, void of compassion, were full of bitterness. These periods of disappointment never really ended, the impact just faded until the next time when it started all over again.

And then I arrived.

The photographs are testimonies to how happy they were. The cards reflect the jubilation that their friends and the rest of the family celebrated. There was a party, a fantastic gathering of all those who had been through it with them. My mother was so very visibly tired, she was so exhausted from the efforts and stress of bringing me into the world. She floated from the car in a state of absolute happiness, banishing the periods of darkness quickly into oblivion. The house was crammed with the neighbours and family. Their old prayers seemingly answered and their new prayers silently asking for me to be protected.

Mrs Davies from next door, sitting in the corner of the lounge and prayed to her Roman Catholic God that I be a good and healthy child. Standing at the door, Mr and Mrs Chan from the end of the road asked their Buddha to create a path of serenity and peace for me to travel while Mrs Siddique, a beautiful covered widowed lady from her place in the armchair by the window asked Allah for his help to keep me safe. With their prayers they bought blankets crafted by their own hands in pale coloured wool to keep me warm, quilts of satin to shield me from the drafts and cotton pillows to cushion my delicate head.

However, despite all their care and concentration, they neglected to seek my protection from myself.

A few days after my arrival, my father with my mother dreamily following him, bore his prize to the house over the threshold and through the hall to the lounge; a true champion. Without saying a word he proudly sat my mother in her chair and placed me into her arms. I was dressed in white, my soft infantile blond hair crowned my head; a golden halo radiating warmth and goodness, it was the perfect picture of a new mother with her new child. My grandparents wept with joy, I would be their last grandchild and their only granddaughter. My father's sister had borne two sons who were five and eight years my senior and doted upon by my grandparents. (My parents ignored the insensitive adoration with dignity, putting aside their own heartache at birthdays, Christmas and other family gatherings.) I was quiet, I gurgled and grappled with the fingers that stroked my cheeks and I made faces at the beaming smiles and adoring stares.

My father meandered around the room to talk to all the guests, accepting their congratulations, their compliments on such a beautiful child and toasts to our doomed future. Someone uncorked the champagne and it quickly bubbled its way around the guests. My mother excitedly took a glass, wonder and pride beamed across her face.

I stared up at her beautifully green eyes that shone with happiness and excitement; an intensity had returned that had been so long missing.

When all had left and a soft darkness descended with the night, my father poured himself a final celebratory scotch and sat himself gently next to my mother who was perched on the bench that ran alongside my cot. They didn't move all night. Each time I woke they were there to feed me, cradle me or soothe me back to sleep. They were bewitched by me as if I possessed some sort of magical power so much so that when the sun rose on the next morning, they were still staring at me, smiling to themselves with their arms around each other, time apparently indefinitely suspended.

I cried and gurgled, ate and regurgitated, slept and crawled my way into their life and they loved me for it. They adored me and I absorbed their worship.

I stop here briefly to catch my breath. The sun is streaming through the roof light in the kitchen, bathing me in a warmth that my skin cannot recall ever experiencing before. Or maybe, I just didn't appreciate it then. I almost feel healthy as I note the tautness of my near translucent skin, pulling across the back of my prominently protruding knuckles, allowing the bones in my hand as I flex my fingers to demonstrate clearly that they still work. My fingers are long, thin, stretching away from the rest of me, slightly wonky in places where they have been stamped upon or have been bent until they could bend no more and then snapped. Occasionally they drag themselves through the fine strands of my lank blonde hair. I can feel the wooden kitchen chair pressing through my fleshless buttocks, my seat bones aching with the constant pressure. I catch a glimpse of my skeletal face in the glass fronted cabinet to my right; my cheekbones announce themselves to the world, the apples of my cheeks long since eaten by the rest of me. My sadness is conveyed by the sheer emptiness in my eyes, fearful at the thought of the promise of the life that I was supposed to have.

Ben had taken over driving from Alex after a brief stop in the afternoon, but he now wearily pulled into an overgrown layby. A decrepit and isolated telephone box was surrounded by nettles, I looked longing at it, knowing that we had no one who we could safely call. With a small sigh, I clambered into the back seat and lay down along the plastic covered bench. Alex got into the back of the landrover and curled up on the floor, leaving the front bench, behind the driving wheel for Ben. A limited of 2 hours sleep before moving on ha been agreed early on. We couldn't take the risk that the landrover wouldn't attract unnecessary attention.

It felt like my eyes had barely shut before the alarm on Alex's watch chirruped shrilly. I had promised myself that because I couldn't contribute to the driving, I would not sleep and would stay awake and help keep the boys awake and alert. So I rose from the bench too and struggled out of the landrover, squatting low and out of sight to have a pee. I breathed in some cold night air, deep into the bottom of my lungs, feeling the refreshment of a slight mist of moisture landing gently on my exposed skin. Finished, I stood up, stretching fingers and arms high towards the black cloudy skies.
"Ready to rock?" Alex popped his head round the back of the landrover, grinning and fiddling at this flies.
"Yip!" I smiled and sprang lightly into the front bench beside

Ben, who as a slow starter was still yawning and blinking hard, trying to clear the sleep away.

"Right, I think we've done enough faffing around. Let's make a push north today." Alex steeled himself, Ben nodded meekly, we'd been on the road for a week and it was telling, but equally so was the fact we hadn't yet been tracked down and this buoyed us immensely.

"So how are we going to get a copy of this tape done?" said Ben.

"Hmmmmm. I've been pondering this. I think we should just transcribe it, and then we sign the document and hide it somewhere. At least that's better than nothing." Alex mused.

"Can't we find a car boot sale or market somewhere? If we can get some paper and pens, we can use the cassette tape in here." I wanted them to show them that I'd been thinking about it too; that I wasn't just a passenger.

"That's not a bad shout. I bet we can get some food and drink too. Just got to find one eh?" Ben sealed the plan.

"Okay, but what are the risks?" Alex injected some caution into the conversation before we get too excited.

"There will be loads of people there, milling around, so we won't look suspicious."

"It'll be cash only, no ability to trace us by cards."

"Cameras?"

"I doubt it- it's so transient that there won't be any guarantee of catching the person being observed."

When I remember times like this, it's fondly, because we did have the occasional bit of fun. These times were a relief, a time when it felt that it was safe enough to laugh and when the fear receded, another feeling filled me entirely. An intense glow spread from my chest, an excitement bubbled in my stomach as I began to realise how precious Ben had become to me. The situation was so serious that I dared not do anything, but it kept me sane, knowing I had that life force within me.

The darkness of the night began to lift as we headed north into Sunday morning, leaving a bright fresh morning in its wake. Rattling along, the landrover was fast becoming our best friend; transport, haven and protector all in one. As we headed northwards we kept watch for signs for Sunday markets. I remembered being taken to one when my parents and I were on holiday once. I think we were in Devon at the time, it was raining and I hadn't been particularly impressed by the quality of the offerings. How shallow that sounds now.

Not without a little difficulty, I pulled a book out from the bottom of my packed bag; the dust jacket tattered and torn to reveal the brown material covering with its gold embossments hiding underneath. The spine, battered but intact, creaked as I prised open the pages, protectively and delicately pulling the fragile pages apart. The front folios opened up, oyster like, to reveal the elegant calligraphy rising from the pages to form the last image in my mind of my grandmother before she passed on into eternity. The words, having never been spoken directly to me were warm, tender but wise and I tried to picture my grandmother whispering them in my ear; so only I could hear them. A collection of poems by a group of English poets, the book itself was a monument in itself, but the fading blue ink manuscript was at the core of the book's significance.

My thin index finger traced the blue ink, following the curves, loops and lines that had been inscribed by my grandmother, and which were already fading from the pressure of my fingers. The circumstances of her ultimate gift were imbedded indelibly in my memory; in the last dignified throes of her life at the Grange, she was sitting in the big dark brown leather chesterfield sitting chair by the blazing fire with the polished mahogany mantelpiece. She was frail, her ageing body beginning to betray and defy her ever youthful spirit but she grasped my small hand firmly. Her fingers were strong within the papery, silky skin from which her blue veins protruded. In the flickering amber of the firelight her eyes seemed to flare with an intensity that I have never seen in anyone since, it was as if a desire to impart her insights had enveloped her, sparking from the light from the fire in the flickering grate. The cancer that had started with her cigarettes was devouring her throat and vocal chords, she was not able to speak and the doctors felt no longer able to assist her save for small comfort.

My parents had left the room to talk to the doctors about Grandma's prognosis. She took the opportunity to give me her greatest gift. After some rummaging around at the back of the settees, from underneath the small mountain of pillows, she dragged the book out. Looking surreptitiously around, she pushed the book towards me whilst pressing her fingers to her lips. She had spotted the bag that I had slung across my body and tried to pull herself towards it. Understanding her immediately, I gently accepted the book and quickly slid it into my bag. My grandmother took my hands in her and pressed them again. We were a picture of true devotion when my parents came back with no clue of the conspiracy between my grandmother and I.

I have read every word of the book countless times, each poem had small tidy manuscript notes and comments; highlighting, musing or questioning the poet's meaning. Like the cancer eating my grandmother, I had gorged myself on the poems until there was no more left, or so I thought. It never ceased to amaze me that no matter how many times I had analysed a particular poem, when I returned something new would reveal itself to me.

We were caught by surprise a couple of hours later with fluttering flags appearing on the left hand side of the road, followed seconds later by a big hand painted sign for a market. A burly man in a high visibility jacket sat in his plastic seat, clearly bored but enjoying the sunshine anyway as we rumbled over the duckboards between the rusting gateposts. The car park was almost full with early birds eager to get the best bargains, Alex swung the landrover into a space near the exit and we jumped out into the ankle height grass.

The market was huge; tables stacked with bric-a-brac, lorry trailers opened to reveal perfumes, electronics or sides of beef; and colourful awnings hiding bras, pants and socks to suit various tastes. With gravel that crunched beneath our feet, we wandered around, gazing at the wares for sale, whilst at the same time searching the faces around us. Ben broke off momentarily to finger some CD's on a stall, I panicked for a second when I lost track of him but he returned bearing gifts; a double cheeseburger for Alex and a bacon and egg bap for me. I didn't care if the van wasn't spotless, nor did it mater if the grease dripped between my fingers, the warm saltiness of the bacon and the runny richness of the egg was food for my severely tested soul.

"That's better- a smile on our faces!" Alex wiped the grease away from his mouth with the back of his hand.

"Yum that was amazing!" I groaned. Ben grinned at me and

my bulging belly flipped over.

"Good, whilst I think this is okay, let's not hang around. I'll go and get some food and drink supplies. Fenn, it'll make more sense if you go get paper and pens. Ben, keep an eye out for us." Alex spoke with an urgent whisper.

"Sure, happy to meet back here at the burger van in half an hour." Ben agreed.

Vulnerability suddenly came upon me as the boys stalked off and I continued to wander casually down the wide aisles. I paused at a sweet stall and snuck glances at the people next to me.- no little wonder that the stallholder was surprised when I got the cash out of my pocket to pay for a giant bag of chocolate bars. On I carried towards a stall a little further down with stationary supplies.

My heart froze when someone tapped me on the shoulder. I spun around on the spot ready to hit, scratch, kick or do whatever to get away so I was taken aback to see an elderly woman holding out a ten pound note.

"You dropped this, m'love." She said in a strong Yorkshire accent and walked away.

I was confused. I had handed over to the sweet stallholder the only ten pound note that I had. I stuffed it into my pocket quickly, "Thanks!" I shouted at her retreating back.

Quickly, and shaking whilst I did so, I found some pads of lined paper and a pack of black biros before heading back to the burger van. I tried not to break into a run but it was all I could do to walk normally. Alex and Ben were standing nonchalantly against the burger van, burgers and chips in hand.

"We're making the most of the opportunity!" protested Ben at the disgusted look on my face.

"At least we got you some too!" Alex joined in.

I smiled with an effort and swapped my shopping bags for the burger and chips. Begrudgingly, I had to concede that it did make sense to get our fill of hot food when we could.

"C'mon, let's go." Ben winked at me.

Back in the musty landrover, I fished the ten pound note out of my pocket.

"What are you doing?" Alex asked.

"An old lady gave this to me- claimed it fell on the ground but I used my only ten pound note a few minutes before." Consternation became evidence on the faces of both guys.

"Let's get on the road." Alex hauled the steering wheel around and backed the landrover out, and after a few bumps and rolls, we were back on the road. Ben watched the side mirrors like a hawk for at least two mils before he decided it was safe.

Carefully, I drew out the edges of the rumpled pink paper, smoothing it flat on my jean-clad thigh.

"What is it?" Alex demanded as his eyes alternated between being the road and the rear view mirror.

The tiny, neat, copperplate writing as hard to see at first, but it was definitely there, written in faint blue biro lines, between the gaps in the pictures on the note. Squinting, I read:

"Glen Nevis, Youth Hostel, Friday, 4:30pm".

I stared at Ben. "It's Sunday today, that's five days away. And we're heading that way too".

"More importantly, how did that woman know we would be at that market?" Ben pondered. "And is it a coincidence that the meet is in Scotland?"

A muddled, fuzzy silence enveloped us as we threw around our worries and questions inside our tired and anxious minds.

"If it was the Guard, they would have arrested us or shot us on the spot." I ventured. "Who would have gone to that trouble to contact us otherwise?"

Was I talking myself into making a mistake?

"Well, we can't keep running and we need to sort out this tape as soon as possible. If we get up there early, we can scope things out and be there before whomever we're meeting. Hopefully that can give us an advantage." Alex decided that we were now on our way to Glen Nevis.

"Okay, let's do it. Fenn, get in the front and start transcribing that tape- we need to make sure we have a copy before any meet."

I dragged one of the shopping bags with me as I hauled myself into the front seat.

For next six hours, I sat on the floor of the landrover being bumped and thrown around, leading on the front seat- no one could see from passing vehicles- clicking the rewind and play buttons on the cassette player frequently. I tried to write slowly and carefully, not knowing who would eventually read it and wanting it to be as accurate as possible.

Chapter 15

My focus on this task was total and so it came as a surprise when we arrived at the Scottish border. I stuffed the pad of paper into the glove compartment and put the radio on. It was early evening and the glowing sun was setting on the horizon.

The border patrol officers wore navy uniforms with the Scottish flag embroidered on the top of the sleeves and were clearly getting ready for some heavy rain with their weighty waterproof coats. A youngish girl with bright orange hair and a face full of busy freckles ducked out of the booth to the right of the car. In a sing song Scottish accent she requested our documentation, bringing her hands to her hip, opening her jacket and revealing her pistol. The Scots had started taking security seriously.

"Passports please."

I dug around in the envelope in my backpack, trying to shield the envelope from the officer's prying eyes. My mouth was parched and my heart was hammering at my ribs. I tentatively handed over Kathryn Walker's passport. The officer flicked through the pages, eyed me up and down, I didn't dare move my eyes away from her hazel eyes.

"Bear with me a minute." She said as she collected the passports from Alex before slipping back into the booth.

"Ssh, keep calm." Ben uttered out of the side of his mouth, into my ear but it did nothing to ease the increasing tension I felt throughout my body, manifesting itself in my white knuckles and the shaking in my legs.

It seemed like time had stopped and we were suspended in a parallel universe where nothing would go forwards or backwards. Sensing my panic, Ben leaned over and took my hand in his, stroking the top of my hand with his thumbs but I was too strung out to take note of Ben's affection. I couldn't hear the drumming of Alex's fingers on the steering wheel and I was oblivious to my foot tapping.

"Sorry folks, I'm new to this job, only started last week and just wanted to check something with my boss." The young officer smiled pleasantly at us.

"No worries, completely understand." Alex smiled charmingly at her.

"Thanks, off you go now. Have a lovely time in Scotland." And with a wave of her arm, we were through.

A few moments passed before we realised we were in the clear and could breathe normally again. The darkness was approaching again but we kept going, looking for less obvious route to get us off the motorway. Now we were in Scotland, the Guard would have far less ability to monitor us but Alex and Be had told me that the President still had a lot of influence in a less obvious and perhaps less official way.

After an hour or so we found a small hamlet a few miles inland of the west coast. It was a bleak place with a bitter wind and icy rain swirling around as the landrover lumbered into an empty lorry park behind a lonely pub. Heads down against the wind and rain, we fought our way into the pub if only to get warm for a while.

The place was deserted which alarmed us- we would stick out a mile- but we reminded ourselves that we were in Scotland where the Guard would be see and treated as an enemy force, if discovered. The question was whether we would be worth the risk?

The barman was a young dark haired man of about 20, who took our order for food and drinks eagerly- clearly we were the pub's only clientele for that day. An open fire flickered and we retreated towards the back of the stone building.
"Hmm, not sure I like this." I muttered.
"I know what you mean. I feel very exposed." Ben mused.
"Well, let's eat, get our heads down for an hour somewhere else and then move on. Glasgow isn't that far- it'll hide us well enough." Alex suggested.
"We only need a few days, if we get to Glen Nevis on Thursday morning, we could actually climb Ben Nevis. At least then we'd have a story for being there." Ben shrugged as he put forward his suggestion.
"Makes sense to me." I was keen just to have a plan.
Alex was about to say something but the barman arrived with our drinks so he smiled and thanked the barman instead.

Our food then arrived and with it a breeze as the front door was pushed back by a tall aging man with wild grey hair and a long grizzly beard. His hands were huge, fingers thick and the skin hardened by work and weather. He nodded at the barman who hurriedly put a pint of dark ale before the new arrival on the bar. The man gazed around the empty pub, his eyes barely registering us bent over our steaming hot but disappointingly tasteless meals, before he perched himself on a rickety wooden stool at the bar.

Our nerves returned, as bad as ever, not knowing who or what this man was. My appetite abandoned me as my stomach tightened and my throat constricted quickly. The atmosphere in the vacant room became heavy and thick stifling my breathing. Alex noticed my knuckles turn white as I gripped my knife and fork harder and harder.

"C'mon Fenn, you really must eat. Everything will be okay, just keep calm." He whispered.

I watched the rain drops trickle down the outside of the steamed up glass window and forced myself to breathe. From out of nowhere, I saw car lights pass by the window and my terror increased, my hands shaking badly.

Clang!

My fork clattered onto the plate. The barman and his sole drinker turned to see what had happened, I froze in alarm.

"It's just a car. We're not in England now, relax and breathe. We'll finish our meal and then leave, okay." Ben leaned into me with a smile.

"Uh huh." I grimaced back at him.

I finished my food by forcing each forkful down, swallowing hard every time. Finally, when the last morsel was gone, we got up from our chairs. Alex and I headed out to the landrover, leaving Ben to pay.

Battling through the muddy car park, heads down again, it wasn't until I closed the door of the landrover that I realised that the car park was still empty. Through the misty glass, I watched Ben traipse across the car park and clamber into the landrover.

"Yuck!" He slammed the driver's door behind him. "You alright?" He turned to look at me.

"I think so. It was just so weird in there."

"I agree, let's move on to find somewhere to rest." Alex said. No one disagreed so Ben started up the landrover to get us moving.

After much discussion we ended up heading straight for Glasgow, to find safety in numbers. Back on the motorway, the bridges and streetlights flashed by. The rain started, stopped and then came down in buckets.

Just outside Glasgow we pulled into a service station and hid the landrover between two articulated lorries. The curtains to the cabs of both lorries were drawn; the lorries had Scottish number plates. Two uneventful hours later, Alex's alarm went off and off we went again. The lorries hadn't moved.

We hid amongst the buildings and people of Glasgow for the

next three days. Multi storey car parks, industrial estates and crowded places seemed to protect us.

Thursday morning found us setting out towards Glen Nevis on what we were sure would be the most important day of our lives. It could change the direction of England or it could plunge us into more trouble than we could imagine.

I could feel the tension and nerves in the landrover; Ben was whistling, Alex tapping rhythms out on the nearest surface. They were the only sounds to break the unbearable silence as we headed ever nearer towards our destiny.

Fort William was gloomy- even at 10:30 in the morning. The skies were a heavy, dull, grey, constantly threatening a barrage of rain. It did nothing to lighten our spirits. We stopped briefly in town to buy the necessities- hiking boots, water proofs, maps, rucksacks- so that we could at least look as if we were genuine walkers. Our cash reserves took a massive hit, which would be a concern whatever happened.

Glen Nevis Youth Hostel was an industrial looking building at the foot of Ben Nevis that had dated unfashionably and uncontrollably. It seemed a practical building, designed like a boot room- brown carpets everywhere and it was busy for Thursday lunchtime.

Optimistically, Alex got us booked in for three nights, thinking it would look odd if we left before the weekend was finished, and we were shown to a room with four pine bunk beds. But, now we were here, we weren't quite sure what to do. We didn't want to draw attention to ourselves, we didn't want to leave anything unattended and we didn't want questions asked.

It was settled when we all sat on our beds and promptly fell asleep. We hadn't had a decent night's sleep since the night before we had set off to meet Stanley. It seemed a long time ago.

When I eventually work, it was eerily dark. I stirred at the sound of voices in the corridor; loud, lively, laughing. They soon passed, returning us to a black silence. I got up and went to the window- I could see the landrover, it seemed fine. The boys continued to snore, loudly.

It felt great to be at peace, even if it was temporary, and I went back to my bed, burying myself under the duvet and letting myself imagine what things might have been like if my father hadn't died; still at school, living at home, university, marriage, kids. Now, I couldn't see anything at all; only a canvas of grey, black, white pixels blurred by uncertainty. My future was yet to be determined.

The voices I had heard in the corridor had been the sound of fun. How long had it been since I'd had fun and really enjoyed myself? I couldn't remember.

I felt a release of tension through my body, like I had let go of myself and it started to spread out on the bed like a puddle. Could I just stay here forever? Please? I knew that wasn't possible.

A distant church bell chimed once, twice, thrice. In just over 12 hours' time, we'd know whether we had been betrayed. I looked across at the sprawling slumbering bodies of the boys- legs and arms hanging loosely over the edge of the bed, poking out of the untidy covers. How easily they slept!!

I was awake properly now and there was little hope of any more sleep. Slowly and silently, I pulled on a jumper and stole out of the room. I crept downstairs through the murky corridors, lit only by emergency lights, creating a greenish hue everywhere.

In the furthest corner of the common room, I found the computer. A small, neat, handwritten note politely asked for donations in an old empty baked bean can. I promised myself

I would do so as I pressed the on switch and hoped that that the computer would be quiet enough. Holding my breath, I listened hard to the silence but I heard nothing.

I logged into my email account quickly, scanning through the boring school notices, ignoring those from Louisa and jumping at the sight of any email from Kate. Taken aback and hesitating slightly with my hand trembling over the mouse, I took a deep breath and clicked to open the email.

It was dated two weeks ago.

"Hi Fenn

I do hope you're okay and you and the boys are safe. This email has taken me a long time to write as I wasn't sure if you'd want to hear from me. I'm sorry that I didn't trust you and I'm sorry if I upset you. It must be incredibly difficult coping with such a heavy burden."

I snorted. How did she think she could put things right in an email? After so many weeks of being on my guard, I deleted the email without reading any further. I wasn't going to be lured into a trap and put Alex and Ben in any more danger than I already had.

With a final check to make sure there was nothing else, I logged out, cleared the cache, switched the PC off and tip toed back to the bedroom. I was completely ignorant of the fact that I had sprung the trap.

I snuck back into bed- the boys hadn't moved at all, to my amazement, letting my eye lids come together, I let my thoughts wash over me and my mind drifted into the ether.

It took me back a few months, and I remembered m despondency at my negligence in failing to give my number to Philip didn't last very long. As I left school on the following Monday afternoon, Philip was waiting at the school gate for me, leaning nonchalantly back on the rail between the school wall and the road. He'd obviously skipped his last lesson to be there on time. My heart throbbed violently and my stomach flipped over and twirled around, I felt I was stepping off a small ledge, about to fall into the dark, blank, endless emptiness below. At the same time and confusingly, my head was light, almost dizzy but racing. I didn't want to appear childish and immature so I strode as confidently as I dared towards Philip.
"Hi." He seemed to beam at me.
"Hi, how are you?" I countered.
"I'm fine, how was your weekend?"
"Great. I didn't do much, you?"
"Dad took me to the Army open day, introduced me to some of

his friends, and had a match on Sunday."

"Sounds exciting. Did you win?"

"Yeah of course, great game, I had a lot of fun."

There was a momentary pause.

"Um, I was …..sort of wondering….if you fancied coming to the cinema with me at the weekend."

Another temporary silence.

"There's a new Tom Cruise film on, if you like that. It's got official approval, of course," He added quickly and hopefully.

"Yeah, that'd be nice, Saturday afternoon?"

"Great, shall I meet you at the bus stop in town?"

"The one on Milford Street?"

"I know it. I think there is a showing at 3. If I meet you there at 2, we can go and get a coke somewhere."

"Okay, I'll see you there." My composure was about to crack.

"Brilliant, see you then", and Philip began to saunter down the pavement. He briefly turned, waved, smiled and pushed his hand through his hair as the sun bathed him in a warm yellow light, and he looked like a divine apparition.

Out of nowhere, the girls jumped out from behind my shoulder, buzzing with murmurs of gossip and chatters of excitement. They demanded to know what Philip had wanted and what he had said exactly. I summarised it all succinctly for them. "We're going to the cinema, next weekend." I was wanted to be Informative, but not give too much information as I wanted to avoid any co-incidental meetings. The chatter became giggling. Mum's car horn broke through the noise, rescuing me from my embarrassing interrogation, allowing me to say a hasty goodbye to my friends; I checked the road and race across to the sanctuary of my mother's car.

As expected Saturday came round slowly. Exams were due to start in a month and our teachers were increasing our workload viciously. Lessons were arduous, tortuous through repetition, words like "exams", "revision", "future" and "failure" used as bludgeons to enforce the idea that work would make you pass. It took me a while to fathom that time would pass more quickly if I just got on with things. But Saturday came round eventually.

I admitted to my parents my interest in Philip. They didn't seem to be particularly happy or unhappy. My father was "worried about his little girl growing up too fast" and my mother was just glad that Philip was tidy, smart, intelligent and of a good family or so his reputation suggested. Conclusions that she had gleaned from the fact that he attended St. Augustine's and which had been confirmed by Louisa's mother at the health spa. The rules were simple; I had to be home by 9.30pm.

Saturday was a beautiful day; bright, sunny with a warm light breeze. I decided to wear my cropped jeans with my white Versace t-shirt, with capped sleeves and a sharp cerise design on the front. I popped on my black Chinese shoes and slipped on my leather biker jacket. I had carefully washed and dried my hair so it lay sleek and straight. My makeup was light and natural and I borrowed my mother's perfume, hoping that I hadn't put too much on in my brief experience. I didn't want to be early, I was aiming for just a little after two but either way the bus arrived at 2pm exactly despite my efforts.

Philip met me at the bus stop just as we had agreed. "Hi you're on time!" He almost sounded surprised. Perhaps he had had the "chat" with his father.
"Oh! I was hoping to make you wait a little bit. You know to be fashionably late!" I tried to sound teasing to hide my embarrassment.
"Didn't work did it!" Philip giggled.
"I suppose not, where are we going for a drink?" I cocked my head to one side, letting my long straight hair swing freely.
"There's a great place around the corner. It does fantastic ice-cream floats and shakes and it isn't far from the cinema."
"Let's go then" I agreed enthusiastically, walking alongside Philip eagerly but leisurely as we chatted casually about our families. Me; an only child, living with mum and dad by myself, I didn't feel that I had much to talk about. Philip had an older brother, called Stan, and they lived with their parents. His

father spent much time away, often for long periods of time. He had visited exotic, remote places with the Army, occasionally taking the family with him.

Under pressure from my intense questioning, Philip described his travels; the differing parts of the dry and arid continent of Africa, varying in temperature, language and tribal attitudes but consistent with its poverty. He had seen the rich opulence of the Oil States, wealth and extravagance beyond the imagination of our citizens all of whom were satisfied with the illusion presented by the Minster for the Economy. I listened in awe to the detailed narrative of the ornate buildings in China, historic and iconic when we discussed them in school. The people were wonderfully different to anyone he had met before; alien at first but fascinating all the same; colour, language and experiences all used in alternative ways. Stan, apparently, had been particularly interested in the politics but their guides, provided (and paid for) by the Army had refused to answer his questions and insisted on remaining faithful to the rigid and complete itinerary that had been carefully and deliberately planned. Philip hadn't been bothered about this form of tour, but it seemed that Stanley had become increasingly and vociferously frustrated at the immoveable refusals to add depth, put context to or colour their visits to historic sites, buildings or monuments that Stanley only interpreted as censorship. His frustration resulted in his disappearances for entire days. Without fuss he would slip off down an alley as they battled through a particularly crowded squared. Sunlight would start to fade into dusky, balmy evenings before he would traipse wearily through the family's accommodation, consumed in his thoughts by sights sounds and tales from the streets, deaf to the urgent pleading enquiries of his mother and angry demands for answers from his father.

Now, Colonel Sanderson attended upon the President occasionally to present an update on the state and readiness of the Army. Philip's mother was the Surgeon General and Dr Sanderson considered all the new research, pored over studies and analysed scientific papers as to new drugs, developments in procedure and progress in practice and would then counsel the President as to his policies on drugs, procedure and practice. Often he would heed her advice, always having listened intently she would say, but frequently she would fail to reconcile her medical knowledge with the ethical, moral and political stance the President wanted her to support. According to Philip, his mother was often left frustrated, belittled and left impotent by these intense exchanges of opinion and when Philip would invite her to tell him she would snap and say that he wouldn't understand. Stanley, Philip's older brother, wasn't around much; he had left home a while back and hadn't been seen since. He was busy with stuff; Philip didn't know what with because Stanley was incredibly private. He had written articles for the local student paper but few had been published and Stanley didn't want his family to read them. Stanley was now 19, had left school at 16 and as far as Philip knew, was working at a local independent book shop called Burtons. It was run by an old Greek man who had moved to Britain after the Second World War. Stanley complained that he smelled slightly of garlic and spoke with an eclectic accent of Anglo Greek with a tang of the East End that Stanley had often found hard to understand.

Alfred was old, stooped but not cowed. I had seen him pottering around his little crowded bookshop as Mum and I passed it. His brown skin had deep folds and his silver white hair sparkled in the sunlight. I learned later from Stan that Alfred had fought in the Second World War against Hitler and his Nazi's and ha lost his beautiful wife Maria to those monsters. I remember thinking and wondering what he would think about the President and whether his sacrifices were a waste.

It was all too much for my mind to sort out its thoughts about Stanley- the one Phillip had told me so much about and the one that I had met a few days ago.

A blast of icy air woke me up brutally and quickly. Alex had thrown open the blue checked curtains and pushed open the window. "Well, the truck's still here"!" He grinned at me.

The door swung open with a bang and Ben came in with a trayful of mugs.
"Here you go sweet pea- good way to get the morning started." He handed me a mug as I pulled myself upright.
"Anyone fancy a walk?" Alex asked.
"Absolutely, looks like a good day for it." Ben replied cheerfully.
I was still half asleep.
"We've got to do Ben Nevis as we're here," Ben started.
"Yep, it'll look off if we don't." Alex finished in any undertone.
They both looked at me.
"Whatever!" I shrugged, taking a cautious swig of my tea.
"Bloody teenagers! Need more enthusiasm than that!!" Alex chuckled to himself.
With a little cajoling and much piss-taking, I was eventually raised from my bed, dressed in suitable clothing and pushed out of the door.

Ben had clearly thought he was being funny; it was grey, damp and grim. The clouds were bulbous, iron grey, blocking out any natural light. My whole body seemed to absorb the moisture, weighing my legs down. I didn't know how Alex and Ben could be so chipper.

"Let's go". Alex set off purposefully towards the footpath and the mountain beyond, shrouded in heavy clouds, giving off a sense of impregnability.

Head down, I plodded after Alex with significantly less enthusiasm than either of the boys. I'd had enough of all of it; my tank was empty.

Ben sneaked up and grabbed my hand.

"C'mon sour puss. I'll get you a hot chocolate when we get back."

"Hmpf" That set the tone for the rest of the hike.

After a tortuous couple of hours climbing rocky step, after rocky step and dragging my increasingly heavy body over each crag, we reached the top.

"Some view." I muttered miserably, staring at the soggy cloudy, nothingness.

Ben giggled. "C'mon here." He pulled me close to him and handed me a steaming hot chocolate from the thermos flask I hadn't know he was carrying.

I beamed at him in surprise. I'd been so pre-occupied, I hadn't seen them put in their rucksack.

A golden warmth seemed to wrap itself around my body and feed itself into my blood stream; with the physical exertion and the hot chocolate, I felt my spirits lift and the weight of my body lessen.

Alex was rummaging around in his rucksack. He pulled out the tape, some plastic bags and some duct tape. I watched him uncertainly, as he wrapped the tape carefully in the two plastic bags and then applying the duct tape. Even if it were thrown into a lock, I doubted that the water would penetrate Alex's efforts.

"I'm sure I'm just being overly cautious, but if this is a trap, I don't want to be caught with the tape. It's too important to lose. We can explain away the transcript as a play I'm working on but we can't explain the tape."

"That makes sense." I nodded.

"There's a cairn over there. I'm going to bury it at the very bottom, that way we'll know where it is."

As Ben and I both nodded in the drizzle, Alex proceeded to carefully dismantle the cairn, digging into the soft peaty earth to bury his bundle of plastic and tape. Almost lovingly, he replaced each stone. Soon it was hard to tell that anything had ever happened.

Remembering a conversation I had had with my dad, I found a large flat rock a few steps off the path and added it to the pile.

"Right, back the way we came." Ben clapped his hands together and grinned manically.

The treacherous descent was slippery but it felt easier, with the sense of achievement bolstering me every step. By the time we got back to the hostel, we had time enough to have a hot shower and get our things together, in case we needed to move quickly.

Rap Rap!

The three of us froze, like weird statues.

Rap Rap! It was a quiet knock, hesitant, surreptitious even. Ben put a finger over his lips and moved slowly and silently to the door.

Rap Rap! The knock has a little more urgency about it. Ben opened the door a fraction. I could see the tension leave his body instantly as he threw the door open wide.

"Lucy!"

"Shhhhh!!!" A short, frizzy haired lady pushed into the room and quickly closed the door behind her.

"I haven't got much time." She whispered.

"How?" Alex started.

"Nevermind, the English Guard knows you're here and they're on their way. You've got to go, they could be here at any minute."

"Let's make this quick." Alex said, digging out the transcript from the bottom of his rucksack.

"We need to get this out into the international community as soon as possible." Ben instructed Lucy.

"Right, what is it?" I looked cautiously at Lucy, she was petite, so her striking red hair made her head look out of proportion.

212

She had an intensity about her that I instantly admired, I could almost see the passion, aura like, around her.

"It's a transcript of a tape, I found, that recorded a visit by the Guard to a farm owned by non-supporters of the current regime. It's evidence of torture and murder." I was surprised to find my own voice as steady as it was.

Lucy looked at me for the first time.

"Oh god." She moaned. "You're Fenn Smythe." Her body slumped. "Oh guys, get out of here now. You can't get caught, not if you're with her!"

We stared at her. Stupefied.

"GO! NOW!" Lucy cried.

The boys grabbed the bags, Ben gripped my arm and pushed me out of the door. We raced to the landrover and scrambled into it, throwing the bags and ourselves onto the floor.

"Stay down on the floor." Alex commanded. Petrified, I was glad to do so. He threw the landrover into reverse and backed out, squealing tyres. It lurched forwards and we sped off.

Very quickly, we were out on the open roads in the Scottish countryside.

Chapter 16

The rain began to hammer at the windows. Despite it being

late afternoon, it was almost as dark as night. A sense of panic radiated between us and our quickening breaths caused the windows of the landrover to steam up.

"I can't see anything!" Alex burst out in frustration.

"Open the window then!" Ben tried to soothe his obvious panic.

I scanned the road behind me, gripping the back of the bench seat so hard my nails hurt, desperate for us not to see anything. The dark clouds seemed to be chasing us.

Through the open window came a quiet buzzing, which gradually became a slightly louder drone.

"What the hell is that?" I asked, panic beginning to torture me now.

"There they are!" Alex yelled.

I caught sight of the helicopter's blazing white lights through the ramrods of rain but there was bang, a flash, thick curdling smoke filled the van with a throttling stench, the van was on its side, flames licked the bonnet and engine. A hand reached in and grabbed my arm, I kicked, bit, scratched, screamed. Ben, momentarily stunned, grabbed my other arm, he began to climb into the back through the seats, trying to get a better hold on me. He slipped, I was distracted and yanked upwards through the open door by the arms and thrown over the shoulders of whatever brute was now encumbered with me. Ben kept shouting for me until a bullet was fired into the van to silence him. I was stunned that this beast could be so callous but could only watch, struggling desperately as the flames consumed the landrover, in an eerie quiet, interrupted by the van's painful crackling and creaking sounds of metal contorting itself. I snatched a glimpse at Alex's beautiful battered face; clearly he'd felt the maximum impact, caused, I could see now, by the neat hole in the front of the van, a missile from the helicopter. The petrol tank erupted with an explosion of fireworks into the darkening and smoky night sky as I was heaved away.

I promised Betty that one day I would tell the truth in my own words, and to this point I have done so faithfully. The difficulty I have from here on is that I don't remember anything with any certainty. It is all hazy, blurred and indistinct. Images flash into my head of needles, bright lights, and white coats amongst vague montages of faces. I remember bouts of excruciating pain but I don't know how it was caused, inflicted or suffered. It just happened. I just felt it.

With this in mind, I will continue.

The landrover was burning brightly and vividly in the dark, as I was bundled clumsily into the back seat of a large car where someone awaited me. My hands and legs were bound by rough hands and clumsy movements, as they pulled my arms behind my back I felt a sharp stab of pain in my shoulder. I had given up struggling at the sight of Ben being shot as paralysis had surged through my body from the shock and terror but now I was trapped, ensnared and panic seeped into the mix of emotions that was pulling me in all directions. I twisted and turned, trying to get a look at my captors but I had been thrown onto my back and could see nothing but the ceiling. Someone pushed my legs back and sat down heavily next to me. A cold eerie calm settled over the car.

"Stop struggling. It won't do any good and it's irritating me."

I felt like I had been poked with an electric cattle prod. It was him, I couldn't breathe and could taste vomit, I felt so sick with terror.

"You are a dangerous animal aren't you? Don't worry, my orders are to bring you in unharmed, undamaged. And I will, but if you continue to struggle, I will happily ignore those instructions. My superiors will accept that you couldn't be contained and had to be shot on sight, notwithstanding the fact that I will make you suffer first. And you know how I will." I could hear the smirk of smugness within the menacing tones and was appalled by the depravity of the man who was evidently enjoying himself watching me squirm in uncomfortable terror. He knew that I had already seen his handiwork. I held myself still to buy myself time, to consider whatever options I seemed to have and to affirm in my mind not to dignify this beast's human status by speaking to him.

"That's a good girl. Now, off for a long trip back to London. There are plenty of people eager to see you! Unfortunately mummy isn't one of them. Did you see her public denouncement of you? No? Ah, never mind. Seems that mummy is now rather ashamed of you. Can't think why? Murder, cavorting with enemies of the state, espionage. Quite impressive for a fifteen year old."

I closed my eyes, gritted my teeth and pulled myself in. I knew it wasn't my fault, it could easily have been me, it was just bad timing. He knew better about that road, he was old enough to know better. I said nothing during the long drive to London through the cold, moon lit night, ignoring the Beast's cruel, taunting remarks and sexual slights.

My fear intensified when he began to remove his gloves dropping them casually at his feet in the footwell of the car. I heard and felt his weight shift against the leather seat. I pushed away from him, my feet levering me backwards until my head pressed against the car door, raised my bound hands over my head to fumble and find the door handle. I pulled, but no, the child locks had been activated. I was completely at this animal's mercy. Of course, he had watched with amusement my fruitless and naïve attempts to escape, letting his cruel giggles linger in the stale, oppressing air. In my frustration, fear and panic I began to cry into my arms that I had dropped into my face. Seeing an opportunity he leaned forward and to my utter, paralysing horror I felt his hands gently caress my breasts. The tenderness of his touch was chilling and repulsed me as he drew a finger over my lips, which seemed to wake me from my succour so that I brought down my arms and began to struggle violently. Violence was met with worse violence and he slapped me brutally across my cheekbones repeatedly before quickly and efficiently in a well-rehearsed movement arranged himself and me into a position whereby he could help himself to my virginity.

It was rough violent sex that hurt. It was so far from the pubescent dreams of first love that I had expected. It was hell's playground; he was the devil and I was his toy. If I screamed, he slapped me, if I tried to bite he would turn me over and try another avenue. He was completely merciless and kept going until I was utterly broken; he would climax, sit back and laugh, wait for his appetite to return and then start again. I lost count after the sixth version of this satanic dance.

I couldn't see much from the car but as the sky lightened with the stealth of dawn, I could see high-rise buildings, elevated roads and the occasional sign to confirm that we were now in London.

We stopped. Not outside the President's headquarters, but outside a normal police station. As the Beast got out, there was an enormous road, flash lights breaking, bodies pressed against the window. The Beast didn't hurry to get me out, leaving me laid out, corpsified, but when he did, he did it slowly. Evidently, the President didn't want to get his hands dirty, preferring the press to do it for him. He nodded at a policewoman who roughly forced me back into my clothes- all the while the door remaining open, me and my humiliation open to the press.

"Fenn! Why did you do it?" Some hack with yellow stained teeth and a steaming coffee bellowed at me.
"I didn't do it! He didn't look before he crossed the road." I would put up a fight, but before I could go on the Beast dug the barrel of his pistol hard into my ribs, pressing me to move forward.

"You've all been conned! I wasn't kidnapped! I ran away! There won't be any reward, it's all lies!" I called, almost tauntingly. The memory of the defiance in Ben's eyes giving me the strength to defy the Beast, knowing that whilst I was in front of the Press I was safe. It was when I was on my own that I was my most vulnerable.

"Shut up!" The Beast hissed. "I will hurt you…… again" He growled into my ear with a smug grin. I kept moving forward towards the front door, wearily knowing there would be further hatred, misunderstanding and ignorance within the hard, concrete soulless box that was the police station. A large broad burly man with stern features in police uniform opened the door as we approached it. He grasped my upper arm, nodded at the Beast and told him "We'll take care of it from here." in rather furtive, sinister tones. He dragged me inside. "Show's over, our turn now."

He forced me to a counter, pressed me hard against it, his weight pushing against me as he untied my hands. The sergeant was leering at me as he attended his counter, charged me with murder by reason of incitement to death - no word from me was allowed- upon which I was led to a cell, small, dark and remote as we crossed a small courtyard at the back of the building to access it.

"Reserved for our special guests." He joked meanly at me, one of the few things I remember with any distinct clarity from this particular period of my life. I stepped purposefully and meaningfully into the dark space. A small glassless window at the top of the back wall, was barred, although not even I would have fitted through it, the door was heavy wood, maybe oak like the ones at school, painted green with an oblong metal hatch. Once I had meekly stepped into confinement, he turned sharply, banging the door loudly and locking it with a clang of finality.

I surveyed my accommodation further, it was sparse with a metal frame bed- the green paint had fallen away years ago- a foam mattress was clothed with a pale thin sheet and an even thinner brown woollen blanket and a flat polyester filled pillow. The bed was pushed into the corner opposite the door and had been secured in the concrete floor, whilst at the other end there was a seatless porcelain toilet and matching hand basin. There was no mirror but a small patched rug that barely covered a third of the cold, hard grey concrete floor, a homely reminder that this was not a holiday. I sank into a freeze of depression and resignation as I lay on the bed and considered the harsh, cruel, reality of my situation. What had I done to deserve this?

I pondered the question itself and the facts that might help me solve this puzzle for the next week or so. Any semblance of time was lost very quickly, my watch had been removed and the gap didn't give much away, day and night were not so different anymore. I felt as if they varied everything deliberately; breakfast, a fibre based cereal with curdling, cloying milk, was often bought at what seemed like dusk. Lunch, only bread and cheese, might be brought with the crowing of a nearby cockerel. If I am honest, I gave up trying to guess, it did more harm than being surprised when the door opened and being pleased to see whatever they brought; it almost created some variety and at times I could see the irritation start to defy their self-discipline. Exercise would involve me being dragged around the yard at a brisk walk with my hands tied behind my back. Occasionally I would fall, trip over, landing on my face, turning it to stop my nose being rammed into the ground. There would then be a huge scuffle and two more guards, one in a white coat, would come running out. A stab in the shoulder as they manhandled me to the floor and hastily bundled me back into my cell.

One bright sunny, fresh day, I think it was early morning as far as I could tell, I clearly recall the light dew on the neatly cropped grass, daisies were starting to unfold, we completed this required rigmarole that they called exercise but rather than head back to the cell, I was lead in the opposite direction to the main body of the police station.

I was taken to a sterile, white room, clinical in its order with the same guard in a white coat on duty. Unusually, and this is why I remember, there was another person dressed in a white coat that was a lady. She had an angelic quality- her shiny dark hair framed her rosy complexioned face. Her pink face shimmered and her round cheeks exuded a kind, softness so that I was reminded of Snow White's motherly nature.

"Hi, how are you?" She smiled brightly through her velvet voice and I began to feel a warmth spread through me, a warmth that I had not felt for a while.
"I'm fine." I was polite, nervous but polite.
"What's the date today?"
"Um, I don't know. My watch has been taken and I can't see the daylight in my cell." I tried to explain myself so that I didn't seem such an idiot. I sensed that it was important to appear lucid and sensitive.
"Can't …. remember… dates" She muttered and jotted something on a notepad. "Fenn, don't you remember?" It was the first time in a long while that someone had referred to me by my name. The pale glow of hope began to rise higher- perhaps someone had realised that this was all a mistake and that I would be released.
"I've lost track of time like I said." I explained, forcing a lid on my frustration.
"Do you know why you're here?"
"Yes. For something I said".
"So you did something?"
"No, for something I said, not something I did."
"Oh?"
"I didn't kill my father. It was an accident."
"Delusional tendencies evidenced by a clear refusal to accept

responsibility for actions." Another note in the notepad and that beautiful, delicate glow of hope was blown away.

"Well, let's take a look at you." She measured my height and weight, listened to my heart, took my blood pressure, flicked through my hair that had grown quite quickly, and then asked me to remove my clothes to check my ribs and stomach.

"Bruises to the forehead and forearms. Evidence of self-harm." She breathed.

"No it isn't. There bruises happened during exercise the other day." I said firmly, wiling the words to be passive and calm.

"Telling lies." She summarised into her notes. Snow White was vanishing before my eyes and being replaced by the Wicked Queen as I noticed the deep wrinkles clogged with make up and the grey hairs that had stubbornly refused to cede to the dark glossy hair dye.

"No I'm not!" The anger was simmering below the surface. My voice was louder, unsteady, suddenly her arm broke free and smashed into the wall. A dozen sirens went off immediately and six policemen swarmed into the room, two of whom pulled me backwards onto the floor so as to leave me stranded, the ceiling looking down disapprovingly at me and I, unable to help myself.

"Thank you, Officers, I think I have enough data now to complete my report on this subject." She nodded sweetly and departed the room swiftly and smoothly leaving me angry at her betrayal.

With the now expected rough and forceful manhandling I was dragged upwards onto my feet with the usual pain to the shoulder- always my right shoulder- and bundled out of the room, but not to return to my cell. I stumbled along the slippery corridor floors, a sharp stench in my nostrils that at first disgusted me and then made me feel ashamed, guilty at the horrible actuality that it was my odour. I caught sight of me in a dark glass; pale, thin, worn like an old doll whose child has now grown up. It shocked me to see my blonde hair, dirty, lank, flat against my scalp growing unevenly since my impromptu haircut. Hollows had moved into the space under my cheekbones, the apples of my cheeks seeking shelter elsewhere. My eyes had been plunged into dark circles and now peered out at the world with fear and discomfort. The greyness of my taut skin exuded a sadness I hadn't felt before, hiding my usually joyful freckles away.

I was delivered to a small close room in which a slight young man was sitting uncomfortably, shifting in his seat with his fear apparent as we approached. I was forced into a chair opposite this man; one of the guards remained on watch in the corner, the rest sneaked out of the room, throwing furtive, suspicious glances at this man and I.

"Right, well, I'm Mr Adams." He said hesitantly, nervously with a slight stammer. "I'm your lawyer for your trial today." I stared at him with suspicion.

He didn't seem much older than either Ben or Alex although there was a world weariness in his manner. A greyness clung to him; his once fluffy blond hair had dulled, his skin drab but worst of all his eyes seemed that they had been emptied of all life, excitement and sparkle. It was as if everything had been erased and his emotions had been numbed. A robot sat before me, his hands shaking and his mind barely functioning.

"Ok, so no one told you that I was coming." I shook my head, not averting my eyes from him; although his multi-coloured patterned tie did its best to distract me.
"We'll have to keep this brief, trial starts in an hour. I've looked at the documents, I think the only option for you is to plead guilty and to get your sentence reduced but it will be difficult in view of the circumstances." My stare began to heat up as a cold fury burst through me, "I will not plead guilty." I said slowly, loudly and firmly as to ensure that there could be no doubt and to indicate that no attempt at persuading me otherwise would succeed.
"Well, I'm afraid I can't help you then." He said evenly with equal certainty that he would not be staying any longer, then closing his briefcase with a final snap and swiftly sweeping from the room. He was followed a moment later by the guard,

the door was locked, to leave me alone once more with only my bewilderment and confusion that he had created and a fog through which I had managed to grasp the fact that I would be attending Court, facing trial without a lawyer and alone. Part of me was maintaining a level of panic that I did not think my heart could healthily sustain, at this thought, another irrational part objected to the cursory way in which this man had assumed it was a case in which a "damage limitation" policy was appropriate. It seemed to me that he hadn't read any documents, merely relied on the purposefully and determinedly inaccurate newspaper stories. His attitude irked me, in citizenship classes, we had discussed how fair trials were important in democracy. I couldn't see anything fair about what was happening to me, the embers of a seething rage were beginning to glow again when the door opened.

"Why can't I choose my own lawyer?" I demanded of no-one in particular.

"You don't get to choose. You gave up that right when you chose to participate in criminal activity. Come on, it is time to leave!" The guard and a comrade lurched into the room and heaved me out of my chair.

"No! Not until I see a proper lawyer!"

Struggling and kicking as best and as hard as I could with my arms bound, they over powered me, the glinting point of needle in someone's hand loomed towards me before I felt the familiar pain in my shoulder and realised that my brief rebellion was futile. I didn't consciously acquiesce to their lugging me out of the room but my resistance seemed to pitter away.

My drifting memory can't be wholly relied upon so I can't say for sure that I was drugged but it seems to make sense of so many things.

With my traitorous strength of will deserting me, the guards quickly seized the opportunity to bundle me through the police station and into the back of a car, waiting in the compound. I was thrown in, guards climbed in on either flank, and the doors locked. Swiftly memories of my last car trip returned and I steeled myself against the expected violation. The car sped away, throwing my head back against the seat, the heavy electric gates opened automatically to reveal a sea of people, parted by figures who protected the road. On the left hand side, people had placards, were shouting, chanting and yelling. I was able to make out their messages of support and allow myself a relieved smile at the possibility that some people didn't want to see me rot in prison forever. On the other side of the divide through which we were travelling, were angry faces, they were abusive, threatening gestures and hateful in their demeanour. A slow rising panic replaced the momentary relief I had felt. Amongst both sides were dozens of flashlights, cameras and video's. Those who had no opinion of me but just wanted shots to sell their papers despite the fact that we all knew the papers would recite the same alleged facts, description and opinions as carefully worded and approved by my mother's colleagues. People were hanging out of windows to catch a glimpse at me, had climbed lamp posts to get a better view and were pressing forward towards the car, curiosity stretched across their faces.

"I've had enough of this. Let's get going!" The guard to my left spat and the driver immediately responded accordingly. The car sped through the crowded streets, and I gazed in wonder at the attention I had attracted. It seemed utterly ridiculous.

The car stopped abruptly, jerking me forward and I was pulled roughly from the car, heaved to my feet and pushed up some marble steps into what I recall was an old Georgian building- one of the few to survive the Purge- three storeys high of white stone, heavy panelled oak doors at each side of which stood two guards actively scanning the baying crowds with grim scrutiny. Inside the air was dark and cool, the marble extended along the long halls, the guards footsteps echoed loudly and firmly announcing our arrival. The long corridor seemed to stretch out before us for eternity, dark oak doors appeared intermittently on our left, while round columns mirrored them on the right with small windows in the wall between the columns. Oak panelling cushioned the walls. I was ready to drop to my knees and let everything wash over me at the point we stopped before the door marked Court 7. My head began to pound instead of my heart, my lungs refused to take any air in, I felt I was suffocating by the absolute fear that had gripped me. It seemed irrational after everything I had seen but I knew once inside no one would listen to me, I would have no say. I wanted to stay where I was, where I knew what was happening, but my body betrayed me by lazily following the guards' lead. The heavy oak door squealed in objection at us and the Court room unfolded before me as I was dragged over the threshold.

A young man of about 30 was sat at the lectern, surveying the Court before him. His long black robes were topped with a purple collar and he wore a white wig, his lap top buzzed fiendishly in front of him, while decrepit books stood earnestly watching over the historic bench.

There was a solitary soul in the public gallery, a petite red haired lady, almost doll like, smartly dressed in a navy wool suite, a small sun shaped badge pinned to her lapel. Exactly the same as the man behind the lectern and identical to the one worn by another lady who was sitting facing the young man. I was taken aback for a moment at so few people being present, after the commotion of leaving the police station, the smallest part of me was slightly disappointed, I wanted my big day in court, but the more rational remainder of me was relieved at not having to suffer this ordeal publicly.

I was directed to a small open cubicle at the back of the room, but in the direct line of sight of the man at the bench whom I now presumed to be the judge.

As part of our citizenship classes we had studied the judicial system; how it worked, the principles behind I and the role in society. Our class was taken to spend a day at the local court to watch some of the cases and to speak to the judges. This all seemed so long ago- it was only last summer when the Court had seemed protective and reassuring but now it felt alien and threatening.

"Fenn Smythe, you are charged with the offence of murder by reason of incitement to death, that on 22 April you said to your father "I wish you were dead." which immediately lead to his death."
"Do you plead guilty or not guilty?"
"Not guilty." At this firm response the judge raised an eyebrow as if this was out of the ordinary.
"Do you have a lawyer?" He asked me directly.
"No, sir."
"Were you offered one?"

"Yes, but he wouldn't listen to me." I answered honestly, sure that the judge would help me.

"Well young lady, you had your chance."

"But he wouldn't present my case; the truth!" I protested.

"That isn't his job. It is not in your best interests, whatever he may have perceived that to be." The judge was firm, his small silver badge twinkling in the sunlight that dropped through the squares of glass in the ceiling. My whole body seemed to sink into itself at this grotesque and perverse revelation, not even the judge was going to be fair and let me have my say.

Whilst the judge spoke to me, two figures slipped between the doors of the Courtroom and into seats behind the red haired lady. I turned to see who these figures were, who would be permitted to attend my trial and was absolutely consumed by nauseating astonishment which was immediately replaced by contemptuous revulsion. I steadied myself against the rail at the front of the box; Louisa sat perfectly demure, attentive to the proceedings, in a black polo neck sweater, black woollen skirt and grey heavy coat. Her mother sat alongside her, wearing a heavy black suit with white shirt. Expensive pearls peeked out from the open collar of this shirt. As polished as ever, her appearance was perfect but did not mitigate the shock of my appearance that was marked all over her face.

I stared because I couldn't do anything else. Louisa dabbed at her eyes with a handkerchief and tried to avoid my eye. Guilt! I made the connection.

The jigsaw pieces in my mind moved swiftly, almost magnetically to reveal what had happened- the stupid silly careless slip of the tongue to Louisa, the footsteps on the stairs and the murky shadows passing underneath the door- all were clues to how I had been betrayed and why I was targeted. I could smell the sour stench of guilt across the Courtroom, over and above the expensive fragrances that they had both drenched themselves in. This foul odour, coupled with their lowered heads and fidgeting fingers in their laps, Louisa and her mother were by their own admission guilty of betraying me.

Despite my best efforts I could not speak, I did not have the requisite qualifications; I should have had a lawyer. And so, half an hour later I was found guilty as charged and on the basis of the Police Doctor's report, shortly after, sentenced to 15 years in a psychiatric hospital.

As I was dragged by the handcuffs from the box, Louisa and her mother stalked out of the Courtroom, the brief moment that the door was open allowed me a glimpse of someone lurking outside the door. My heart audibly broke for the second time when I realised it was Philip and saw him comfort Louisa in his arms. Oh! Could that ever have been me!

Chapter 18

The next 15 years are a vague blur of pain, hysteria and numbness. I cannot remember specifics, and to be honest I do not want to try, my mind has locked these memories away for ever for a reason. I can, however, summarise this period of my life quite succinctly. I was kept in solitary confinement for eighteen hours everyday. The six hours for which I was released were taken up by breakfast, lunch, exercise but mostly by group therapy, I was restricted to reading state sponsored comics and could not have access to any writing materials. I was denied access to television, telephones and computers; I was banned from all forms of communications.

And so here I am, sitting at this table. As far as I can tell, from the limited access to newspapers and television reports that I have been permitted, the situation has not changed since my release. The trials of those supposed silent assassins like me are not overtly reported in the media, instead heard by judges in quiet solace with a single reporter to make their report for posterity alone but without the due process of a fair hearing. The Social Worker shakes her head at me, slowly almost sadly. It is clear that she doesn't think I'll improve sufficiently to become re-integrated in society; her conclusion is right but for the wrong reasons. It isn't because of the amount of time I have spent locked away from society, it is because I feel that society at large has betrayed me and that feeling of despondency is now coupled with my only purpose left; to make things change. The quiet shy person I became to complete my sentence may remain as a withdrawn individual who is afraid of the world, according to the Social Worker, and to a certain extent I may accept that situation. The Social Worker raises herself slowly from the chair, picking up her bag from the floor as she rises and heads of out of the room without even a goodbye. That was our last session.

With a stiffness that I doubt will ever leave me, I rise from my chair and limp slowly across to the kitchen sink. There is a frozen feeling in my knee which means it no longer bends as freely as it once did- much like me, I suppose. There is a puffy swelling around the knee cap, protecting whatever damage was done to it by the many beatings. I gaze out of the window at the yew tree in the back of the garden, my eyes rest on the small neat bird box. A little robin flits from the fence, landing on the top of the box and positioning itself to survey the garden. It almost stares back and I know the tape is safe.

Now that the haze of government induced confusion is clearing I can see that I am now 30 years of age and have seen more in my life, both inside and outside of the hospital in the State's attempt to beat every piece of individuality out of me, than most of the people in this country. People who live in blind but comfortable ignorance that has been created by decades of lethargy. How did we get to this?

The turbulent conundrum is raging and tumbling around me so that a big part of me is glad that I have suffered because I have seen the truth, the reality and I have finally recognised that none of it matters. The harder part is that no one will believe me because it is too late. The President has obtained credibility by virtue of his length of office, being held criminally accountable for your thoughts is now widely accepted by the populace at large in this country including those like my mother who were, should have been, clever enough to see this coming.

A huge part of me died, that night in the car. I will never be 16, never date and never share my life with someone. The slope was slippery but it was made greasier by the poisonous mixture of power, greed and ignorance so that climbing back to where we came from now seems impossible. But perhaps my small spark of hope that refuses to be extinguished can join with others to start a great fire that will consume all before it and give us all a fresh start. A question- how many of us and how long will it take?

Will you join us?